The Shelby F. S[
BOOK C

The
COMPLETE
Adventures of

# SHELBY F. SQUIRREL

and Friends

Eleanor Lawrie

# Credits and Acknowledgements

Front Cover Design: Birgie Ludlow

Special thanks to Photographer, Tony Pratt, for his beautiful portrait of the flying squirrel for 'Shelby Meets His Match'. Please be sure to visit his amazing website: tonypratt.com

Other Photos and Images: dollarphotoclub.com

Thanks also to Michael Robinson, for his help in developing the plot for 'Shelby Meets His Match'

ISBN 9798389874381
Copyright © April 2014, March 2015

For Kira,
my beautiful daughter.

# The SHELBY F SQUIRREL Series

*As your child grows, so does Shelby!*

**BOOK 1**
**The Complete Adventures of**
**SHELBY F. SQUIRREL and Friends**
Age 4-10  (Shelby is 3 months old to 2 years)

**BOOK 2**
**The Great FOREST CAPER**
Age 8-11  (Shelby is an adolescent)

**BOOK 3**
**Where is Virginia?**
Age 9-12  (Shelby, an adult, is now a father)

Visit Eleanor Lawrie at flutesandflyingsquirrels.com
Email:  eleanorlawrie1@gmail.com

# Contents

## Part Two: Shelby on the Farm

*Soon he was on the edge of a parking lot behind a tall building that seemed to stretch all the way to the sky.*

# SHELBY'S FLYING LESSON

Shelby F. Squirrel was so excited he was quivering all over! His mother had just told him that he was old enough now to go down to the ground with the rest of the family to hunt for fallen nuts. He and his twin sister, Darby, were not babies any more!

"But," his mother had sternly added, "You must never go down to the ground alone! We always go together."

The other thing their mother had told them was what the initial "F" stood for. He and Darby had always wanted to know, but were told that they would find out when they were older.

She had patiently explained, "You know that other squirrels look a lot like us, and behave like us most of the time. Our tails are shorter and our fur is thicker, but the most important thing to know is what our middle initial stands for. It is the same for every member in our whole family." She paused for a moment and taking a big breath, announced, "Shelby Flying Squirrel and Darby Flying Squirrel are your full and proper names, and in a few days you will have your first flying lesson!"

"Oh, no!" cried Shelby. "I'll never be able to do that, I just know it!" and before either of them could stop him he scrambled down the tree and across the grass.

Without looking back, he just ran as fast as he could and soon he was on the edge of the parking lot behind a tall building that seemed to stretch all the way to the sky. As he glanced around he was startled to see a small black and white dog come trotting toward him. A low growl came from away down its throat and it suddenly dashed right toward Shelby.

Shelby's little feet skidded on the pavement as he took off, but he skittered toward the door that someone had just come through and darted inside before he even realized what he was doing.

He was in a small room with no way out! There were two shopping carts in the corner and a closed door on each side wall. Straight in front of him was another different looking door. He was in a complete panic, eyes popping, chest heaving, when the different looking door slid open sideways! And then another door slid open just a little bit in front of that!

In a shot he was through them both, and went sliding across a beautiful room with soft furniture, carpets, and potted plants. He sat back on his haunches to take it all in, his head turning in all directions. There were big windows that gave a view of greenery and flowers. Shelby thought it was the most wonderful sight he had ever seen! He decided to do a little exploring and began tiptoeing about. He had only gone a few inches when a man appeared from the hallway that ran off to the left side of the room. The man had a lot of keys that jangled. The sound made Shelby nervous, so he sat up to see what would happen.

That's when the man saw him and, letting out a huge yell, leaped toward him. Shelby didn't know what to do! He was trapped for sure! And then an amazing thing happened. The wall near him started to slide open! In a twinkling he tore through the opening. He banged into a wall inside and felt quite dazed. As his head cleared, he realized the whole little room he was in was moving! A few moments later, the motion stopped and the door rolled back.

Out like a blue streak went Shelby! It was the right thing to do because, just as he escaped, two little elderly ladies stepped into the elevator. That was a stroke of luck, for sure. Neither of them noticed him, and the door closed leaving Shelby in an empty space with two hallways running off in opposite directions. Now a second panic attack gripped him. He saw no way out. Not a scrap of daylight peeped through anywhere. Shelby dearly wished he hadn't run away from his mother and sister like that. What a dumb thing to do! He curled up in a corner and started to cry softly to himself. After all he was not much more than a baby, really.

Oh, no! The sound of footsteps snapped him out of his gloomy mood. He peeked around the corner and saw that a door had opened a few feet away. A man had already come toward the elevator and was waiting for someone else to join him. Shelby raced past the man, and dashed through the door just as a lady came through, and it swung shut. He felt a lot safer in here. At least there was daylight! He nearly lost it entirely when a big furry cat leaped at him from the chesterfield, missing him by a whisker. He went instinctively toward the window, which was also a door!

Through that door, gasping for breath, scuttled Shelby. He circled around in a pretty tight space before jumping up to get away from the cat. He found himself on a ledge looking down at the *top* of a large tree!

That's when something magic happened. He didn't even have to think about what he was doing. He just threw himself off the ledge and in the direction of the tree. His little legs stretched out as wide as they could, and on each side of his body the loose skin miraculously became a parachute. But more than that, it was a parachute that he could steer! By tilting his tail a little he controlled his flight and landed perfectly on a branch that gave gently with his weight and swayed for a moment while he caught his breath.

Shelby F. Squirrel was down that tree, across the grass and back up his own tree so fast that he almost became a blur. His mother and Darby were waiting with frightened looks on their faces.

Taking huge hiccupping breaths, Shelby stammered, "Oh, Mother! Oh, Darby! I can fly! I can fly! I did it! And I promise to listen to you from now on! No more running away for me!"

*"What do you think you're doing?" It was an enormous black bird, with a mean look in his eye. "What kind of silly animal are you anyway?"*

# MOVING DAY FOR SHELBY

"Shelby! Darby!" called Mother F. Squirrel. Her twin children were playing tag in the big tree where they lived. They came slipping and sliding along the branch where their mother waited for them. Mother let a moment pass for them to catch their breath before speaking.

"Children, I have decided that we need to move," she began.

"Oh, no!" wailed Shelby. "I like it here and I am just getting to know where everything is!" Darby looked rather nonplussed but was quiet.

"No, I've made up my mind and there will be no arguments!" answered their mother. "There are fewer trees around here every day, it seems. Yesterday a huge machine moved into the bush beside us and men with saws got out and started to cut the trunks on the biggest ones. Soon there won't be enough of them for us to safely fly back and forth."

With that she gave them instructions to gather up two cheekfuls of nuts to take with them, while she would do the same. They would be hungry when they found a new home and probably wouldn't have time to look for any supper. Signalling for them to follow, she climbed to a high branch and soared downward to the next tree.

Darby was right behind her and Shelby brought up the rear. They went quite a long way in this fashion, and then Mother stopped and turned around to face her twins.

"We should keep going in this direction, but

we need to cross this big, busy street to get to those trees on the other side. I need to think of a way to get over there." It was a bit difficult to understand her with the two cheekfuls of nuts, but she spoke slowly and they nodded at her to show they understood.

Shelby looked around quickly and excitedly started to chatter, "MFFP! MMMF!" he hiccupped as he tried to speak. Mother and Darby just stared at him, their eyes wide.

"Shelby, take some of those nuts out your cheeks! We can't understand a word you're saying!" said Darby, and Mother came closer to hear him better.

"Okay, there," he said, carefully putting a couple of nuts beside him on the branch, where they wouldn't roll off. "Look, down there! That nice-looking lady is helping those children cross the road. Maybe we can run really fast and get over there with them!"

"What a good idea, Shelby!" said Mother. Shelby felt very happy when she said that. "We'll need to get closer and then run for it at just the right time. Follow me and don't do anything original. Darby, you stay behind me and then Shelby will come after you. We better stay very close together. Okay, let's go!" And she started going lower on the tree trunk until they were together on the far side of the trunk about six feet from the ground.

"Now!" she whispered, and scampered quickly toward the sidewalk. Darby and Shelby were close enough to be her shadow. The crossing guard lady had raised her sign and was waving a group of children across, while several cars stopped and waited. Mother and Darby were already on the opposite sidewalk when a big ball came bouncing toward Shelby. One of the children had dropped it and now was chasing it, with the crossing guard lady holding her sign high, hoping the cars would keep waiting. Shelby did a U-turn to avoid being knocked over by the ball, and when he turned back, Mother and Darby were gone!

Shelby panicked and ran as fast as he could toward the sidewalk and up a tree. He kept going all the way up, up, and then came to an abrupt halt. There was no more tree to climb! He had climbed up a telephone pole! He froze, not knowing what to do next. He nearly fell off the pole when a raucous voice shouted at him.

"What do you think you're doing?" It was an enormous black bird, with a mean look in his eye. "What kind of silly animal are you, anyway?"

"I....I....I'm a squirrel! A flying squirrel!!"" he managed to blurt out between hiccups, remembering to speak carefully around his stuffed cheeks. The big black crow let out a scornful squawk.

"What? Do you think you are a bird? Oh, brother, now I've seen everything!" and he moved closer. "Let's see you fly, then!"

Shelby didn't wait a moment longer. He scurried partway down the pole and found the nice-looking crossing guard lady standing at the bottom looking up at him.

"It's okay, little fellow," she said in a soft

voice. Shelby understood immediately that this was his chance and that she was protecting him. "Come on, you can do it."

He glanced upward to see where Darby and Mother were, and slipped and slid down that pole like there was no tomorrow! He ran faster than he had ever run before and almost flew up the trunk of the tree where they waited.

They didn't waste any time, but just climbed up really fast to fly to the next tree. There were many more trees in the direction they took and they got safely to a lovely forest before it started to get dark. Mother took her time to pick out the best one to use as their nest tree and they carefully took the nuts out of their cheeks, choosing one each to eat right away.

The F. Squirrel family slept soundly that night in the new nest. Shelby dreamed of rolling balls and big black birds, and said a grateful thank-you to the nice-looking crossing guard lady who had helped him in his moment of need.

*The eyes looked so steadily at him he was mesmerized by them.*

# SHELBY IN THE DARK

Shelby F. Squirrel and his twin sister, Darby, were just waking up from an afternoon nap. As they slowly stirred and opened their eyes, they realized their Mother was quietly sitting watching them. From the look on her face they both knew she had something important on her mind. It seemed every other day that a new lesson awaited them, now that they were old enough to learn the ways of all flying squirrels.

"Well, you two slept quite a while!" said their Mother eventually. "Are you both wide awake now?"

Shelby and Darby sat up straight and tried to look attentive, the way good children should look. What they really wanted to do was go and play tag in the treetops. It was their favourite game now that they were such good fliers.

"It's time, children, for you to take the next step toward becoming *adult* flying squirrels!" said Mother with a note of pride in her voice. After all, they had done very well so far, even though they were both still quite young.

"It's a good thing you had such a long nap, because tonight we start flying in the dark, like true flying squirrels. We are much more comfortable at night, because......."

"Oh, no!!!" wailed Shelby in a piteous tone, interrupting her very rudely. "I know I can't do that! No, I just can't do that!! I....I.....Mother, Darby, I'm *afraid of the dark!"* he hiccupped and started to cry. He was so ashamed! He had never told anyone before! But there it was now, totally out in the open.

Darby humphed and said, "You *can* do it! Mother knows what is best for us, so just stop your whining and decide to be brave!" Darby was much too wise for her age, and so calm in the face of all these scary things. Shelby admired his sister a lot, so he took a deep breath and turned toward their Mother to listen.

"When the sun sets, we will begin," she said sternly, and that was that.

Shelby was getting more and more nervous as the rest of the afternoon wore on, and seeming much too soon, there was his Mother signalling him and Darby to come with her. She motioned them both to come out of the old woodpecker hole that was their home.

Shelby held his breath and did what he was told. He looked around him and discovered he could see amazingly clearly. He glanced at his mother and saw the humour in her eyes. "Have you never wondered why our eyes are so large?" she queried. "The other squirrels don't have such big eyes."

"Oh," squealed Darby with delight. "I always wondered why! Now I finally know! That's so awesome!"

There was a full moon shining down as they climbed up their nest tree to begin to fly. As they went higher and higher Mother kept a close watch on both of her twins. Shelby was trembling all over, but now it was from wonder at the beautiful scene before him as well as from fear.

Then suddenly they were alone. And there was Mother sailing downward in a graceful arc toward a nearby pine tree. Darby gave Shelby a shove and he lost his footing and was floating, floating through a misty, unreal world. His natural instincts took over immediately and he landed quite expertly close to his mother. In about two seconds Darby was beside them. All three of them began to look for small pine cones to nibble and soon the quiet night separated them.

Then, "Whooo-oo-ooooo!" came a ghostly whisper from just over their heads. Shelby nearly jumped out of his skin. "WHOO-OO-OOO!!" much louder and longer came the sound.

Darby pressed tightly up against Shelby's shoulder. They huddled together the way they had when they were babies. Then in a flash, they took off running along the branch toward where their mother was, feet scrabbling on the rough bark.

"Who-ooooo!" startled Shelby so much that he lost his grip completely and was falling, spinning toward the ground. Then suddenly he was flying instead and firmly attached to a new branch, staring into the brightest, sternest pair of eyes he had ever seen.

The eyes looked so steadily at him he was mesmerized by them. Then they were gone; then just as abruptly they were there again!

"Goodness gracious! Haven't you ever seen an owl before?" the creature asked.

"N-n-no, this is my first night out in the woods with my *family!*" squeaked Shelby, trying not to hiccup. He stressed the word *family* so the owl would know he wasn't alone. "H-h-how did you do that with your eyes?" he couldn't help asking, even though he knew it wasn't polite.

"I'll show you!" and the owl turned his head so far to the left that Shelby was seeing the back of his head, then a split-second of the straight-ahead stare, then the face shot around to the right, giving Shelby another view of the back of his head!

"Oh my, that is so amazing! Your head looks like it could unscrew!!"

"I think it is pretty wonderful myself, and I still remember my mother explaining why I could do that!" said the owl. The look in his eyes was much more kindly now, and nowhere near so staring.

Shelby was beginning to feel a little foolish. Then the owl spoke up again, "I decided to give you a little lesson, and I hope it has helped you to realize that you are perfectly designed for night flying. I am truly sorry if I frightened you too much, but did you notice how you flew without a problem in the world when you weren't thinking about it? You *can* see and you *can* fly at night! And you are much more ready to be an adult flying squirrel than you give yourself credit for!! They don't call me the Wise Old Owl for nothing, you know!" And with a great whoosh of his huge wings, he was gone.

Shelby could see Darby and Mother nearby, and he felt so much better! This was going to be just fine after all!

It was all white and had dark eyes and the most amazing long ears that flopped all about.

# SHELBY'S NEW NEIGHBOUR

Shelby F. Squirrel woke up from a really long afternoon nap. He had been snuggled up against his sister Darby on one side and his mother on the other side, so he was all cozy and warm. The days had become much colder lately and when it was time to sleep, the three of them had to curl up in one big furry mound to keep from shivering. Darby and Mother showed no sign of waking up so Shelby stretched and yawned and decided to go outside for a bit of air.

He noticed that there was a hush that he wasn't used to! And the opening of the woodpecker hole seemed almost to glow. Shelby moved slowly and tried not to disturb the sleepy-heads as he detached himself from the tangle of legs and tails. When he was sure they were still sound asleep he went straight for the opening and looked out.

What a shock poor little Shelby had then! He rubbed his eyes and looked again. He thought he had lost his ability to see. Those wonderful big huge eyes failed him for the first time!

But wait!

"I can see everything here inside our nest!! It's just when I look through the hole to the outside that all of a sudden I can't see!" Shelby breathed to himself. And with that he started to look more carefully into the strange solid whiteness before him.

Slowly, very slowly, shapes started to form and he knew they were the trees that he was used to. But they were all covered in a thick layer of white! A hazy sun was lighting up the scene. Shelby couldn't see the ground at all!

"Oh, boy," said Shelby, "I want to find out what that stuff is!" And gingerly he stepped out onto the big flat branch in front of the nest hole.

"Brrr!" he took in his breath sharply at the coldness that wrapped itself around his legs. He quickly looked down and he couldn't see his feet!!

He was standing in a soft layer of fluffy white material that was FREEZING COLD!! When he got more used to the coldness, he took a few steps along the branch.

Shelby gradually was getting used to the almost completely white world facing him. He decided to go up higher in the tree, realizing he had better go quite slowly, which was very difficult for a young, healthy flying squirrel like himself.

Up, up he went, slipping here and there but managing to continue upward without any major catastrophes.

Soon he was up to the level he usually would fly from to get to the next tree. He sat there and began to think. He knew there was a pine tree with lovely swaying branches, so he carefully checked until he was sure he recognized the shape. Yes, he could see shadows under the limbs. Maybe it would be a good idea to go higher, though, to give himself more distance to steer on the way down and over.

So up he went to get a better take-off position. Every branch was covered in white and under the soft fluffy stuff, the branches were glass smooth and even colder! At last, Shelby decided to fly down to the pine tree. He pushed off in his usual way, but he felt his feet slip as he let go.

"Oh, no!!" wailed Shelby as he spun out of control. Desperately he clutched at a branch as it loomed near. He got a grip, but immediately started to slide along and was soon mid-air again, spinning downward, out of control.

He grabbed for another limb but it was too slippery to stop his momentum. He felt himself land on the top of a branch and just dive right through it to the next one. And the next one and the next one and he kept falling!! Down he plummeted through flakes of white and pine needles.

Then with a great WHOOSH, he stopped falling and found himself in a heap by the trunk of the pine tree. As he sat up to take in a breath, it suddenly became darker and with a loud THUMP, clumps of this terrible white stuff fell on top of him and kept falling until only his head was sticking out!

Shelby cried out with all his strength, "Mother!! Darby!! HELP!!! HELP ME!!!"

It seemed that his voice didn't leave his mouth! Everything was so heavy and hushed that the sound became muffled and he thought, "Oh, no! They can't even hear me!" And he started to cry and hiccup all at the same time. He was a very sad little flying squirrel who wished with all his heart that he had stayed in that warm nest hole.

"Well, well, what have we here?" said a voice sharply in his ear.

Shelby stopped crying and hiccupping in the middle of a gulp and stared into the face of a new creature. It was all white and had dark eyes and the most amazing long ears that flopped all about.

Now it was hopping madly in a circle and loudly proclaiming, "Here we go again!! Another kid out in the snow without permission! Now stop your whining and listen up! This is called snow. SNOW! Got it? It's the same as rain except in winter it is called snow!"

With that this strange giant-eared animal shook out a huge back foot and began to dig Shelby out! He turned his back on Shelby and dug and dug and sent up great plumes of snow until Shelby was free again.

Shelby started to hiccup again as he tried to say thank you.

"Now, never mind, I'm just being a good neighbour! I move into this forest every winter and now here I find you half buried. But now you're okay and you need to go home and learn how to manage in this weather! Tell your mother the Snowshoe Rabbit rescued you!" And off he hopped into the whiteness of the woods.

Up Shelby climbed back into the safety of home. Mother hugged him for a long time and said, "Oh, Shelby, Shelby, come and get dry and I will tell you and Darby all about what happens in winter in the forest!"

*The animals pulling the sleigh were long-legged, and mostly brown and looked a lot like the deer that sometimes grazed in this very field.*

# SHELBY'S FIRST CHRISTMAS EVE

Shelby F. Squirrel and his sister Darby were playing in the forest one night after a hunt for food with their mother. They had become quite adept at getting around in the snow by now and set off to the meadow at the edge of the woods. It was a little bit foggy and they liked to play tag on the ground for a change, especially in fog because they liked the out-of-focus feeling that the fog made.

As they came closer to the meadow they heard sounds that were out of place in the forest. First a sharp whistle, then several more, all with a downturn at the end. Then a great WHOOSHING sound, followed by tinkling, silvery ringing. They hurried to the edge of the field just in time to hear stamping of feet and a big, bass "Ho, ho, ho!"

They stopped at the edge of the grass, and stared at the scene before them. It was a roly-poly man with a long white beard, wearing a red suit with a black belt and black boots. He was riding in a huge sleigh and an enormous bag sat behind him.

The animals pulling the sleigh were long-legged, and mostly brown and looked a lot like the deer that sometimes grazed in this very field. In a few seconds they were loosed from their straps and began wandering and feeding, chewing at the grass that was just below the snow.

Then one of the lead animals was suddenly closer to Shelby and Darby, causing Shelby to take in a sharp gasp in alarm. The big breath made him hiccup loudly, upon which the creature swung his head and looked straight at Shelby with big inquiring brown eyes.

The most mysterious thing about him was his nose. It was decidedly red! And it was actually glowing in the semi-dark! Shelby started to hiccup in earnest, he was so excited and afraid all at the same time.

"What kind of noise is that?" asked the animal. "Who made that noise?" And he came much closer bending his head to see better.

"Oh, that's just my brother hiccupping!" offered Darby, always able to keep much calmer than Shelby. "He hiccups when he gets excited or scared!"

"Well, you have nothing to be afraid of," said the creature.

"Who are you? And why is your nose red and shining like that?" said Shelby, forgetting his manners altogether, he was so curious, and ending up with a resounding "HIC!"

"No, you first, tell me about yourselves!!"

"We're squirrels," they both chorused.

"Squirrels hibernate in winter! Why are you not sleeping?" was the response.

"We're - HIC! - flying squirrels!! HIC! - We don't hibernate! And we're nocturnal, we - HIC! - like being awake at night!" hiccupped Shelby.

"And we're twins," added Darby. "Now it's your turn!!" "Okay, then. My name is Rudolph, the Red-nosed Reindeer. All these other reindeer and I pull Santa Claus around in his sleigh every Christmas Eve. I get to lead because of my red nose, especially on foggy nights. We stop here every year because of the tender grass for a short break. I think I better take you to see Santa now, what do you say?" He bent his head really low to the ground and said, "Hop up and hang on to my antlers, they're a lot like tree branches so it should be easy for you." Up they jumped and Rudolph raised his head slowly and trotted off toward the sleigh. The red-suited round man watched as they approached and smiled with a warm twinkle in his eye.

"My, my, we have visitors!" he exclaimed. After introductions done smoothly by Rudolph, he stated firmly, "You need to know more about me, I think. Well, every year on this night I travel all over the world and deliver toys to children. This big sack on my sleigh is *magic* and it never gets emptied no matter how many toys I take out of it. Let me see now, I wonder if I can find something in it for two little flying squirrels!"

With that he turned his back and started rummaging in the sack. He grabbed at things and tossed them aside, muttering to himself, "No, not that! No, not that!" as he went. Then he stopped digging and turned around with his hands upturned, and came back toward Shelby and Darby and Rudolph. His eyes gleamed with satisfaction.

"Look! These are pecans, from Alabama, and these are macadamia nuts from Hawaii. Here are some lychee nuts from China! And these are Brazil nuts - the name will tell you where they are from. And this is the reindeers' favourite lichen, from the nearest trees to the North Pole!! And here are some dried cranberries that are especially sweet!"

He handed the treats to Shelby and Darby with a great flourish and watched happily as they stuffed everything into their cheeks.

Shelby started to dance up and down and was soon hiccupping all over again in his effort to say thank you to Santa.

Darby composed herself and said very slowly, around the full cheeks, "Oh, thank you so much! We'll share these with our mother and remember this night forever!"

It was time for the team to continue on its journey, so Santa gathered all the reindeer from their grazing and soon had them properly hitched into their harnesses. He jumped into his sleigh and gave a loud whistle, followed by more, all of them with an upward turn at the end.

Shelby's and Darby's eyes got bigger and bigger as the sleigh lurched forward and, after one really long whistle, left the ground in a cloud of snow and jingle bells.

"MERRY CHRISTMAS!!" they all heard Santa yell as his sleigh and the reindeer disappeared into the fog. What a story they had to tell their mother this time!

*"Stop that, you crazy animal! You're covering me in snow! Stop it right now or I'll knock you right out of that tree!"*

# SHELBY GOES FOR A RIDE

It was a beautiful afternoon!  The sun was shining on a fresh layer of soft white snow, making it glitter brightly.  As was so often the case, Shelby was wide awake when he should have been snoozing after the usual evening food hunt and the early morning forage through the forest with his family.  Darby and Mother were all bunched up together, fast asleep,  and didn't stir when Shelby crept out of the nest hole.

He slithered down the trunk and jumped into the perfect clean snow.  He burrowed into it and stuck his nose out, leaped high in the air, and then did it again.  What fun!!  Then he decided to climb the evergreen tree and started jumping from branch to branch making showers of powdery snow spray every which way.  Then suddenly in mid-flight, a loud voice boomed through the air.

"Stop that, you crazy animal!   You're covering me in snow!   Stop it right now or I'll knock you right out of that tree!"

Shelby missed the branch he was aiming for and flew downward out of control!  Smack!!  He landed on something firm, high off the ground, gasping and hiccupping and hanging on for all he was worth.  He found himself looking straight into a large disapproving eye, and heard the booming voice again, but this time it was right there in front of him!

"Well, well, would you look at that!  It's a rat and it thinks it's a bird!!" and then the strange beast started laughing so hard it nearly shook

Shelby off his perch. The laughing went on, whinnying and neighing something awful.

Shelby started jumping up and down, shouting through a dreadful case of hiccups, "I am (HIC!) not a rat!! (HIC!) I am not!! No, (HIC!) I am not a rat!!" until the laughing stopped abruptly and the huge eye was examining him again.

"Well, explain yourself, then! What on earth are you?" he was asked, rather imperiously.

"A squir(HIC!)rel!! A f-f-flying (HIC!) squirrel. And I was just (HIC!) playing in the snow! I didn't mean to throw snow at you!! (HIC!) I didn't even know you were there!" he stuttered out. "Who are you, anyway, and what are (HIC!) you doing here in the forest? I never saw anyone who looked anything like you before! (HIC!)"

"You have never seen a horse before?? What kind of a sheltered life are you leading, anyway?" and again that whinnying, neighing laugh echoed through the trees. "Well, I am here with this big sleigh attached to me to give some people a winter sleigh ride through the woods. They have left me here while they gather some branches for a bonfire tonight. You should be more observant, you weren't paying attention at all!" He snorted derisively. "Lucky for you that I am a friendly animal, isn't it?"

Oh, boy! Shelby felt so ashamed, and so told off! He hung his head and said in a rather shaky voice, "Oh, yes! I was just having so much fun! I forgot to check that I was safe! Oh, oh, oh!" followed by a series of hiccups, and looming tears.

"Hey, it's okay! No harm done! You'll

remember from now on maybe. I can see you are pretty young, and you still have a lot to learn! Tell you what, would you like to go with us on the sleigh ride?"

Shelby thought about that for a minute, and nodding, answered, "Oh, yes, I would, I would! But, will you come back to this part of the forest to bring me home?"

"As ordered, young fella, you can count on me to do just that! But first I want you to run up home and invite your family to come with us. Here come the people and they will want to get going, so hurry!"

Shelby turned to go and found Darby and Mother looking into his face from the nearest pine branch. Oh, no, now he was in trouble!

But instead, Mother grinned widely at him and said, "It's okay this time, Shelby, let's all go together. I know this horse from when I was about your age. We are old friends! Hey, Charlie, how are you? You sure got Shelby with your nonsense! A rat indeed!! You haven't changed a bit. I would know that laugh of yours anywhere!"

There was plenty of room on Charlie's broad back and they were soon on their way, with a merry group in the sleigh behind them. There were bells on Charlie's harness and they tinkled with a silvery sound as he clip-clopped along.

It was an afternoon the F. Squirrel family would remember fondly for a long time. Of course, Mother and Darby always reminded Shelby of how reckless his behaviour had been that day, and how upset he had been when Charlie called him a rat.

But the main thing was that Shelby had definitely learned a lesson. Yet another one!

*There was a sweet smell in the air that he found intoxicating, so he decided to get closer to see what it was.*

# SHELBY AND THE SUGAR BUSH

It was a beautiful, crisp day in winter, with a hint of spring in the air. The sun was shining, the air was clear and Shelby was in the mood for adventure. He was tired of always telling his mother where he was going. He and Darby knew the trees between their nest hole and the meadow inside out and backwards by now. Shelby decided it was time to see what was in the other direction.

As so often happened, Mother and Darby were fast asleep, and Shelby was wide awake. It was early afternoon when he crept out and quietly climbed to a high vantage point. Off he leapt with a wild abandon that felt new and exciting. Off on his own, he thought, this should be absolutely great.

He had floated through three or four trees before he started to wonder if he truly could keep track of the route he took. He glanced behind him and it all looked like alien territory. "Oh, no!" he cried to himself, alarmed. "This going solo might not be such a wonderful idea after all."

He sat for a while and worried about what he should do. Then, in typical Shelby fashion, he decided to keep going and figure out how to get home later. So onward, tree after tree he went, a little flying squirrel, finding out that the forest around him was a lot bigger then he had previously thought.

After a few trees had gone by, he started to enjoy himself, despite knowing deep down that he was actually lost. Sooner or later he was sure he would find his way back. He kept on doggedly, until he spotted some buildings in the forest.

There were thin strands of smoke wafting up from some of them, and a group of children standing around listening to a big person tell them a story. There was a sweet smell in the air that he found intoxicating, so he decided to get closer to see what it was. He slowly came down the trunk of the tree he had landed in, hoping it was thick enough to keep him hidden from view. He got to the ground and very carefully peeked out toward the activity.

Just then, a line of children started coming in his direction, carrying plates piled high with pancakes and swimming in maple syrup. He stayed out of sight, absolutely frozen behind the tree. Suddenly there were children on both sides of him, carefully balancing their plates and heading for the picnic tables a few feet away. That was when total bedlam broke loose.

The nearest child tripped on a tree root, falling forward and tossing his plate in the air as he fell. The plate bounced once and managed to stay upright on its edge, and began rolling toward Shelby!

Shelby dodged to the other side of the tree trunk but couldn't go further because another child had stopped to try to help his friend. So as Shelby spun around in terror, shaking all over, the plate rolled right into him and knocked him flat on the ground! Poor Shelby was covered in maple syrup and the whole world suddenly went all dizzy and weird.

Shelby was too dazed to object when he was

picked up gingerly, tenderly wiped off with a paper napkin, and then gently turned over and set down on the ground. Coming to his senses enough to realize he was in a very sticky situation, he blinked and tried to get his bearings. Overhead there was a wild, high-pitched stream of chattering that was somehow familiar. Looking straight up, he could see his mother and Darby running back and forth on a branch safely out of reach of the people, calling to him to run up the tree.

He barely made it to their branch, he was so out of breath. They continued to chitter at him in a rather scolding tone.

"Oh, Shelby, you had us so frightened there! Whatever were you thinking to go down to the ground like that, when you know it is always so dangerous?" his mother asked. "Don't you remember anything I've told you?"

Shelby wasn't interested in answering her questions. He had a couple of his own. "How did you know where I was? How did you find me?" he stuttered, hiccupping as he spoke. "Boy, am I ever glad to see you!"

At this Darby finally had her moment to speak up. "I saw you go off all on your own! You went up the neighbouring tree from our nest, and flew away exactly in the other direction from way, way up high. I called to you but you couldn't hear me, so I followed you. Mother saw me go and came really fast behind me."

"We saw everything," his mother broke in. "If you had not been so absorbed in your naughtiness you would have heard both of us

45

yelling at you to stop, but, oh no, you were deaf, that's for sure."

"Now follow us home and don't you ever do that again!" she said in a very stern voice. With that she began to climb up chattering loudly as she went.

Shelby Flying Squirrel felt sure he had learned his lesson. A very ashamed and sore little squirrel went to bed that night and dreamed of being lost in the woods. In the morning he went to his mother and gave her a big hug.

"I love you, Mother," he said in a quiet voice. "I'll try really hard to be good from now on."

...it was followed by a head with two bright, glittering eyes that were wearing a mask! It was a round grayish animal, with a fluffy tail that had large black rings around it.

# SHELBY DOES A GOOD DEED

It was a clear evening and the F. Squirrel family was sitting on a pine branch not far from the nest. They were contentedly munching on some lichen they had stripped off a nearby tree trunk. Suddenly their senses came to full alert, when there was scuffling down below them, and deep male voices.

A few seconds later a sort of parade appeared in the open space between the tall trees. There were three men carrying what looked like boxes, but the sides of them weren't solid. Shelby thought he caught a glimpse of movement in one of them.

Mother signalled him and Darby to stay still and keep quiet, so they watched as the strange scene unfolded.

There was a bit of discussion between the three men and after some moments, the three boxes were placed on the ground in the middle of the little clearing. Each man fiddled with the end of his particular box and stood back, making a quick visual check on the surroundings.

"They should be safe here," one of them said. "Looks pretty quiet right now." With that they all trooped out of the glade and disappeared from view.

Shelby held his breath, knowing he had to prevent a hiccup attack! Who knew what was in those boxes? All three flying squirrels stayed absolutely still, eyes glued to the forest floor.

After some rattling noises, with the boxes

being shaken about quite a bit, the end of one of them dropped open and a sharp nose poked out into the night. It was followed by a head with two bright, glittering eyes that were wearing a mask!

When the rest came out, it appeared as a round grayish animal, with a fluffy tail that had wide black rings around it. The unusual creature quickly moved to one of the other cages, which was actually what the boxes were, and juggled and wiggled and uttered little squeaks, until the end of the cage dropped down and out came another one that was just the same, but a bit smaller.

The two of them now hurried to the third cage and opened the end with no trouble. They were fast learners, that was obvious. Out of the last cage emerged two roly-poly miniature versions of the others. They snuffled each others' faces and necks for a few seconds, seeming glad to be together, safe and sound. Then they waddled off a bit awkwardly, slipping into the darkness of the evening.

Shelby and his family darted back to their nest, wondering about what they had witnessed. They settled in for a snooze to be ready for the next hunt through the trees for food.

"Hey!" a rather gruff voice shook all three of them awake. "Come up here and take a look, this would be a good nest!" And then a sharp nose poked its way into the opening of the old woodpecker hole, eyes quickly darting around.

Mother F. Squirrel answered calmly, "I'm sorry to say, but this is our nest. You have to find another place!"

By then there were two masked faces filling the doorway, whiskers quivering.

"Oh, my!! Excuse my bad manners! I am Ringtail Raccoon and this is my mate, Lottie. We had a nice place to live in the city but were trapped and brought here. We're just looking for a new place to live. Our twins are Molly and Polly. Come and say hello, you two!"

Two miniatures of Ringtail and Lottie appeared in the nest opening, whereupon the F. Squirrel family was properly introduced. And Shelby broke in eagerly, with a hiccup, "I know a place! I know a place! (Hic!)"

So began an eerie procession through the forest, the three flying squirrels gliding from branch to branch, Shelby in the lead, with the whole raccoon family trying hard to keep up as they trotted along on the ground. Shelby led them to a huge fallen oak tree that was mostly hollow and sat back while the strangers wandered into the opening, pushing this way and that, with little happy squeaks from all four of them.

Just then one of the little raccoons suddenly jumped off the end of the nearest branch, and landed with a plop on the ground. She lay sniffling loudly and woefully.

"Whatever made you do that?" said Ringtail, running to help. "Are you okay, Molly? Speak to me!!"

"Oh, Papa, I was just trying to fly like Shelby and Darby and their mother. I want to do that, too! It looks like tons of fun!"

With great patience, that surprised the F.

Squirrels, Ringtail explained to Molly, "You can't fly because you are a raccoon! Raccoons don't fly! Birds, bees, butterflies and flying squirrels fly but raccoons don't fly, Molly!"

He continued, "There's nothing wrong with being what you are, you know. You are a perfectly fine raccoon and Shelby is a perfectly fine flying squirrel. You can still be friends. You don't have to be exactly the same to do that!"

"Am I ever glad you didn't try that from higher up, Molly!!" hiccupped Shelby happily. "We'll have lots of fun playing in the forest, don't worry about that!"

And all four youngsters were soon romping around, both in the trees and on the ground.

Mother F. Squirrel smiled warmly at Ringtail and Lottie and said, "Welcome to our little corner of the woods. I'm so glad Shelby noticed this old fallen tree and remembered where it was. Good for you, Shelby!"

Oh, Shelby literally glowed as they all joined in to agree with her. He thought, *I could get a real swelled head after this!*

*The children wandered off through the trees.*

# SHELBY GOES TO SCHOOL

Shelby F. Squirrel was dreaming that the forest had been invaded by small creatures on two feet with little piping voices. He woke up feeling a little alarmed and stretched carefully so he wouldn't disturb Darby and Mother. It was mid-morning and sunlight was streaming through the hole in the tree into the nest. To his great shock he discovered that the dream wasn't a dream after all! He could still hear the babble of voices from below!

He went to the opening and looked out. What he saw made him pull his head back inside with a jump and a small hiccup. Several children were standing in a circle, with four adults over to one side. Then the children were hushed up by one of the adults and Shelby had a feeling of deja-vu when the next voice began to speak. He knew that voice!! But from where? And from when?

In a few moments the children wandered off through the trees. Shelby hopped out onto the flat branch in front of the nest hole and looked down. Then he peeked back inside to see whether Darby and Mother were still asleep. No sign of them waking up for quite a while, he thought. He sat there and wondered what was going on in the forest today.

Shelby and his family had been on a very successful food hunt the night before, so he shouldn't have been hungry for a long time. But something was making his mouth begin to water. He realized it was the tantalizing aroma floating up from the bottom of his very own tree!

When he scampered over a bit further he could see there was a lumpy looking sack of some sort leaning up against the trunk.

"Oh, boy, that smells so yummy!" he said to himself. He sat still for a minute trying to decide what to do. That delicious scent was driving him crazy!

Shelby slithered and scrabbled down the tree and put his nose into the bag. He put his whole head into the bag. He got his two front paws into the bag, then his shoulders, then, KERPLOP, he landed at the very bottom of the bag!

He soon found what was smelling so delicious and irresistible. It was a bag of peanuts! Shelby tasted one and liked it a lot, and in about five minutes he ate the whole bag. After that he felt so-o-o-o sleepy. His head started drooping and he fell fast asleep.

Shelby was dreaming that he was moving along in a swaying motion that made him feel a little queasy. He also dreamed that he heard the little voices again. Then the bag sat still and suddenly he was wide awake.

"Oh, no!" he thought, "not again, this is really happening! And where am I?"

With that he slowly stuck his head out of the bag and what he saw caused him to start hiccupping totally out of control! He was in a roomful of children, with a few adults. Before he could hide inside the bag, a shrill voice shrieked, "Oh, look, look, there's a mouse in Andy's knapsack!!"

Shelby hiccupped and started to cry, he was so frightened. Someone was hushing the children and the room became quiet.

One of the adults spoke next. "I am going to zip the bag shut and take it outside, and then I will open the bag and let the mouse go," said the eerily familiar voice. And with that came a loud ZZZ-I-I-I-P and the swaying motion started again. Shelby started to listen as he was swung along. The nice voice was so calming.

"It's okay, little fella, I will let you go over at the edge of the trees so that you can run into the woods away from the playground. Then you will be absolutely safe. I just hope you can find your way home from there!" said the voice.

Then the bag was put gently on the ground and the zipper slowly opened. He timidly poked his head out of the bag.

"Oh, my, I've seen you before!" said the kindly, soft voice. "You aren't a mouse! You're a little squirrel, and I believe you are a flying squirrel!!" It was the nice-looking crossing guard lady!!!

She carried the bag with Shelby in it over to the edge of the woods and looked into the trees. Sure enough, peeking out through the leaves were two other flying squirrel faces. In a flash, Shelby saw them too. Mother and Darby!! He nearly fainted with relief!

"Well, little fella, there you go!! Your mother and sister are up there and now you will be fine. Off you go, off you go!" said the crossing guard lady in her gentle way.

Shelby ran and ran and climbed, crying and hiccupping as he went. Up, up to where Mother and Darby were waiting for him. Darby spoke first, not without an unmistakeable amount of frustration in her voice.

"Oh, Shelby, you are impossible!!" she began her tirade. "Honestly, when will you learn to be more careful?? What if the children were from another school that was far away? We would never have found you!" Soon she was crying too, at the thought of it. Mother hushed them both up with a stern look.

"Just get control of yourselves, you two!" she said, with a resigned sigh. "It's lucky for you that we both woke up in time to see you in trouble again and were able to follow. Let's go home and then we'll talk about learning how to be responsible!!"

Shelby didn't know what that big word meant. But he knew for sure he was going to find out very soon.

*She told Shelby that one of her wings was injured but thought it would be fine with some time to heal. But she needed to get up that tree and knew she had to have assistance.*

# SHELBY TO THE RESCUE

One day in the middle of May, Shelby was playing in the tallest pine near the meadow. He was flying from branch to branch and seeing how fast he could land, scramble back upwards, fling himself off again and land again in the same place.

He was feeling pretty smart-alecky about himself, creating all sorts of world records in his mind. Off he leapt, using his feet as a springboard, and flew even faster toward his target. Before he could get there something soft and light was in his way for a tiny instant. He felt a light brushing come in contact with his outflung tail. When he landed with a sinking feeling, he quickly looked behind him and below him was a small, spinning object, spiralling out of control toward the ground.

"Uh,oh!" he piped as he made his way down to see what had happened. "What was that?"

When he got to bottom of the tree, he hurried over to the small heap on the ground.

"Help me, can you? Somebody help!" emerged a chirpy voice from the dishevelled pile.

"Here I am!" answered Shelby breathlessly. "Are you okay?"

He was looking into a rather accusing eye, which was quite obviously sizing him up. "I am so sorry! I didn't (hic!) see you!" now Shelby was starting to get upset. "Tell me (hic!) what I can do to help!"

"I need to get back to my nest! I need to sit on my eggs!! They'll be getting cold by now, so I have to get up there!!" babbled the hurt creature.

It took some explaining, but before long Shelby learned he had narrowly missed a real tragedy by almost colliding with a mother robin while she flew toward her nest. Actually, she was a mother-to-be, because her eggs still had not hatched. She told Shelby that one of her wings was injured but thought it would be fine with some time to heal. But she needed to get up that tree and knew she had to have assistance.

Quickly Shelby told her to grab onto his tail with her beak or her feet, and he started to pull her slowly toward the tree in front of them. He was going to need help to do the whole job, though.

"I will get you to that first low branch where you can feel safer and a bit hidden" he puffed as he crept up the trunk, "but I am going to get my sister and mother to help get you all the way up there."

The poor little robin huddled there and waited while Shelby hurried off. She shivered and thought she would never see the little flying squirrel again. He was too young to really appreciate how much she needed him. She was never going to get up to her eggs!

But she should have had more faith in Shelby, because in no time at all he was back and had two other lovely helpers with him.

"Okay!" Shelby explained, "If you can keep hanging onto my tail the way you did to get this far, then Mother and Darby will each hold onto one of my front feet as I climb. Are you ready?"

So the strange group began its ascent, inching carefully toward the robin's nest. Each time Shelby had to move one of his front feet,

Mother or Darby would hold it and help to pull his passenger with him. With a fair amount of puffing and a few inevitable hiccups, they found themselves at the robin's nest, no worse off except for their hammering hearts.

In two quick steps the robin was on the nest and settled herself over the pale blue eggs, with a huge contented sigh.

"Oh, thank you so much, thank you!" she exclaimed. "please allow me to introduce myself now that there is time to talk. My name is Rosie. My mate, Rusty, and I go south in the winter, and we just got back here a few weeks ago. You weren't living here last year, were you?"

So Shelby introduced his family and they told Rosie how they came to be living in this particular forest.

The whole Flying Squirrel family kept a watchful eye on Rosie, observing that Rusty brought her an endless supply of worms and insects to keep her fed. Then one day he flew onto the branch in front of the squirrel nest and announced that the babies had arrived.

They all admired the pitiful scraggly baby robins and laughed to see how they did nothing but keep their beaks as wide open as possible waiting for food! Rosie's wing was still a little sore, so Shelby took care every day to help bring tidbits for the hungry crew.

It was wonderful to hear the robins' beautiful songs every evening and morning, and know they were going to be friends for life.

*He looked down and saw a tiny creature with a very long skinny tail, little round ears, a pointed nose, long whiskers and piercing eyes.*

# SHELBY GOES CAMPING

There had been a lot a strange noises coming from the meadow all afternoon, but Shelby had resisted the urge to investigate. He had forgotten about it in the meantime.

Now it was evening and the F. Squirrel family was out for the first hunt of the night. As they drifted down toward a favourite tree near the meadow, they all suddenly sat bolt upright on the branch where they had just landed. There was an orange glow coming from the meadow! When they went cautiously a little closer they saw it was a big fire with people sitting around it in a circle. And they were singing, and shoving long sticks into the flames, then eating the blob of gooey white from the end of the sticks! Thoroughly confused by what they saw, the F. Squirrels retreated to their nest to have their own evening snacks.

Shelby awoke early after another hunt through the forest just before sunrise. He crept out of the nest in his  well-practised way, without disturbing Mother and Darby, and in no time at all was sitting upright on the edge of the meadow, his nose and ears twitching as he took in the scene.

A lot of boys and a few big people were busily going in all directions. There were tents, piles of wood,  picnic tables,  all in what seemed like utter chaos. Shelby was quite mesmerized by it all. He didn't know what to make of it.

"Hey!" a voice squeaked from just below him. He looked down and saw a tiny creature with a very long skinny tail, little round ears, a pointed nose, long whiskers and piercing eyes. "Who are you? Even better, *what* are you?" it squeaked again.

"Oh! Oh!" mumbled Shelby, trying to organize his thoughts. "I - I - (hic!) I'm a squirrel. My name's Shelby F. Squirrel. Pleased to meet you! (hic!)" He was trying to remember to be polite.

"Well, hello then, Shelby F. Meet Marvin F. Mouse! Glad to know you, I'm sure. We have the same middle initial! Are you a Field Squirrel? I bet you are, I bet you are!!"

*Oh, here we go again,* thought Shelby. *Nobody has ever seen a flying squirrel!*

But he explained patiently to Marvin about his own F. Marvin's face changed from OH! to WOWIE!! as he listened.

"What a team we could make, Shelby! You want me to show you what this bunch of stuff in the meadow is all about?"

First they went into a tent with rumpled-up sleeping bags and clothing strewn all around. Marvin explained that this was a Scout camp and they were here every June on the second weekend. They scurried out of the sleeping tent just as two half-dressed boys popped through the flap, too busy chatting to notice the little animals.

"This is the most important place to know about!" squeaked Marvin. "It's the cook tent, and we can find lots of good things to eat. Just don't knock anything over or there will be trouble for sure!" he warned.

They crept into the tent through the flap that

acted as a door. "Follow me!" said Marvin. And he climbed up onto a shelf with boxes and packages piled high on it. He chewed with rapid tiny bites into one of the bags and soon light brown flakes were spreading on the shelf.

"I love this taste! It's called oats," said Marvin, sounding even more squeaky as he nibbled furiously. "They cook it and eat it in the morning." Shelby agreed that it tasted wonderful and dug right in.

Neither of them noticed that the bag was starting to lean over, and suddenly it toppled, teetered a moment, then plunged headlong over the edge of the shelf!

C-RRRR-ASH!!!! The ruined bag of oats landed on a pile of huge cooking pots and knocked everything every which way! Just as Marvin had predicted, the sound of running feet was heard immediately and shouting voices came nearer in a flash.

The two new friends streaked for the door, veering sharply around the edge of the flap exactly as the first person dashed inside.

"Shelby, help me get away!" screamed Marvin. "They'll step on me! Oh, HELLLP!" With that he leaped onto Shelby's back and hung on for dear life.

Shelby's feet barely touched the ground, while he headed for the first tree at the edge of the meadow. Without looking back, he scrabbled up the trunk, his claws slipping badly because of his passenger, who was tiny but was extra weight nonetheless.

Huffing and puffing and hiccupping to beat the band, Shelby paused for a few seconds on the first limb. Then, steeling himself to be strong, he quickly climbed to a higher branch and with a whisper to Marvin, "Hang on TIGHT!" he leaped into space.

"Hey, hey, we're flying!" yelled Marvin in Shelby's ear. "I think I'll change what my middle initial stands for from now on! Marvin *FLYING* Mouse; what do think of that?"

And Shelby thought it was just fine with him! No doubt he and Marvin F. were going to be fast friends for a long, long time.

*Nobody wanted things to change, things were just fine right now, thank you very much.*

# SHELBY AND THE MEADOW MYSTERY

It was pretty early in the morning but Shelby, Darcy and their mother were already finished their predawn forage for food through all their favourite parts of the forest. They had ended with the beechnut tree near the meadow and all three of them realized at the same time that something was going on over there. Without any discussion about it they moved closer to the edge of the trees and looked around. They saw a group of people with shovels and large bags. They watched for a few minutes but nothing seemed to be happening. There was just a lot of talking and pointing, so the F. Squirrel family went off home to take a nap.

The only problem was Shelby couldn't sleep. Not when there was such a mystery over in the meadow, so as soon as Darby and mother were obviously sleeping, off he went to see what he could see.

This time there was organized activity for sure. The people were spaced out across the meadow, each one dragging a bag and using a shovel. The routine was to reach into the bag, pull out a small bit of something green, then wedge the shovel into ground. When the ground was pushed open by the shovel, in went the little green spray, out came the shovel and down went the person's heel onto the spot, flattening it out.

Then after taking careful strides forward in a matching line with the other people, the whole process was done over again. What were they doing to the meadow?

"Does anyone know what this is all about?" a voice sounded close to Shelby's ear. It was the Snowshoe Rabbit, looking very different in a coat of brown fur. "This looks like an invasion to me!"

Ringtail Raccoon said in his rough way, "It's an invasion, all right! Way too many people for my liking!"

"It looks like they are putting something in the ground," said his mate, Lottie. "Every time they move forward, they have to take another whatever it is out of the bag."

"But what?" chimed in someone above their heads. There sat Rosie and Rusty. surveying the scene from a higher branch. "We need to know what it is, don't you think?"

Shelby said, with a hiccup, because this was upsetting him for some reason, "I sure want to know! We love the meadow! We play here almost every day, and what about the Scout Camp?"

"And Santa?" cried out Darcy, who had just arrived. "What if Rudolph can't land here on Christmas Eve?"

Suddenly there was a flurry of steps down below and a piping shrill speaker said, "Oh boy, they better not mess with my meadow, that just can't happen!" It was Marvin Field Mouse, hopping from foot to foot in quite a frenzy. "I'm getting really scared that this is a bad thing!"

Then, rudely from much higher up, came a voice Shelby remembered but not fondly. "Who cares?" it was the big, black crow that lived near the school. "Just find other places to play or

74

whatever! Grow up, for crying out loud!!" and he flew noisily away, much to everyone's relief.

Nobody noticed with the flapping of the crow's wings that someone else had arrived, so when he said, "WHoooo!!" they all nearly jumped out of their skins.

"Calm down everyone, calm down, let's try to figure out something to do instead of just weeping and wailing away here!" It was the Wise Old Owl. And right behind him was Shelby's and Darby's mother. She sat beside the big bird.

"There is only one person I know that I could ask and that is Charlie. Do you want me to go and get him?" she asked.

An immediate chorus of yeses and nods sent her on her way, and they settled in to watch while they waited.

The line of people in the meadow had reached almost to the centre of the field. It didn't look different, only if you really squinted could you see little dark marks where the shovels had gone in. Still it had everyone from the forest worrying and wondering. Nobody wanted things to change, things were just fine right now, thank you very much.

After a while soft clip-clop noises were heard and Charlie's laugh came through the trees, with its usual whinnying, neighing sound. He quieted down as he got near enough to see into the meadow and everybody was afraid to breathe.

"Well, I happen to have worked a whole summer dragging bags just like those and piles of shovels to fields and hills for miles around. It was a long way from here, where I used to live," he said slowly.

"Tell us, tell us!!" they yelled at him.

"Okay, don't get yourselves all worked up! What they are doing is planting trees…."

"Oh, come on, look! Those aren't trees! They are too small!" protested Shelby, with echoes from the others.

"Yes, they are, even though they are tiny. They are called seedlings and will grow into trees, so that in a few years, there will be a forest there instead of a meadow. It is done to replace trees that are cut down for logging, to make furniture and build houses."

And so it was decided, that everyone would move to the forest beside Charlie's farm and soon plans were being made for the stages of the move to take place. Yes, there was adventure in the air. A whole new life awaited the F. Squirrel Family and their friends and neighbours.

# PART TWO

## SHELBY on the FARM

It had a big curved tail with feathers that swooped upward in a graceful arc and then separated as they curved back down, flopping grandly. Its head was quite small and had red quivering decorations dangling from it, both on top and under the fearsome looking beak.

# SHELBY AND THE SULTAN

Shelby was pretty tuckered out after all the excitement of moving to the new forest by Charlie's farm. The forest friends had all decided to move now that the meadow was newly planted with seedling trees. There would be plenty of lovely fields to play in on the farm.

The beech tree with the old woodpecker hole that their mother had chosen was close to the edge of the woods, with a view of an orchard and a barn just between the next row of trees.

The F. Squirrel family had hunted more intensely for food during their night forays after arriving yesterday afternoon, to have some extra for storing away. Darby and Mother were fast asleep and Shelby shook himself awake, crawling slowly out into the early sun.

Just then a piercing cry cut the quietness of the air. Shelby nearly jumped out of his skin! He had barely started to breathe more normally when it happened again! It was coming from the farm.

He peeked inside the nest and saw that Darby and Mother had not stirred at all, so what else was a naturally curious flying squirrel to do? He set off to find out the source of the loud calling cry, even as it rang out again.

He didn't have to go far, just a quick fly to the next tree, then one more and then down the trunk for a dash across to the orchard on the other side of the fence. The last tree in the orchard gave a clear view and the sound was right in front of him now, so he climbed into the branches among the apples and started to look more carefully.

It was a bird!! A big one! It had a big curved tail with feathers that swooped upward in a graceful arc and then separated as they curved back down, flopping grandly. Its head was quite small and had red quivering decorations dangling from it, both on top and under the fearsome looking beak. The legs were yellow and quite sturdy with visible sharp claws. The feathers on its breast were glossy and changed from green to black to blue all at once as the sun glanced off them.

This awesome critter was sitting on the fencepost just a short distance from Shelby's tree, and soon it yelled powerfully yet again, "Cock-a-doodle-doo, and good morning to you, too!"

Shelby just had to get a bit closer. After all if the bird was yelling "Good Morning" at the top of its lungs it must be friendly.

Shelby went to the fence and climbed up a post to say his own "Good Morning". He had just drawn in a big breath when the bird suddenly shot straight toward him along the top of the fence, half flying and half running.

"Weasel! Weasel!" it screamed even louder than before, "To the henhouse, ladies, get inside, get inside!" Then it pulled up short and stood surveying Shelby with sharp beady eyes.

"Hic!" was all Shelby could muster, he was so shaken by the threatening look on this bird's face. "Hic! G-g-g-ood m-m-morning! Hic!" Oh, this was not going well! If only he could quit these annoying hiccups.

"Hey, you don't look like a weasel, now that

I look more carefully. What are you, anyway?" asked the bird, changing his demeanour quite abruptly.

"I-I-I'm a squirrel!" stammered Shelby, very intimidated by now. "Hic! I just moved here from another forest!! Ask Charlie, ask Charlie!" Oh, thank goodness he had the wits to remember that Charlie had said to mention his name to anyone on the farm to ensure a welcome.

"Oh, of course!" said the bird, backing off and looking apologetic, "Charlie told all of us there would be quite a few new friends coming to live in this forest. Sorry if I scared you, little guy, but I have a job here! I have to keep the hens safe to wake everyone else up in the morning. Just doing my job!"

"All clear, ladies, all clear!" he suddenly screeched, nearly knocking Shelby off the fencepost.

He seemed to have second thoughts, then said more gently, "Well, I guess introductions are in order! My name is Sultan. Probably got that because the farmer likes to refer to the ladies as my harem!" He laughed uproariously at the joke, but Shelby didn't know either word so he just stared at Sultan feeling very naïve. His mother would know, he thought, making a mental note to ask her later.

He realized Sultan was staring back at him now and stammered quickly, "Oh, s-s-sorry, it's my turn, isn't it! M-my name is Shelby F. Squirrel and the F stands for 'Flying', and I live with my mother and my twin sister, Darby. N-nice to meet you!"

Wow, he made it without a hiccup and

privately hoped that meant he was outgrowing the nuisance reaction he had so often.

"Flying?? Flying?? I saw you run up the fencepost, why didn't you fly up it if you can fly?" Sultan wanted to know.

"No, no, no, we can't fly like birds can, but we are really good at floating through the air. In fact, we can get to places pretty quickly because we can do that!" Shelby explained, with more patience than he felt.

Just then he noticed Mother and Darby watching from the last tree in the orchard so he waved them over. After more introductions all around, Sultan took the whole family to meet his harem, and on the way home Mother explained what the words meant.

Shelby was feeling quite proud of himself for the success of his encounter, but Mother soon made it clear that she was getting tired of his habit of getting into hot water because he kept going off on his own.

So poor little Shelby hung his head and vowed to be more accountable in future.

By now he was absolutely positive about the location of the yummy aroma, and quickly climbed down onto the railing, and across it to where two round dishes were sitting in the shade of the tree.

# SHELBY BURNS HIS TONGUE

Shelby had really thought it would be easy to behave himself in the manner that his mother expected him to, but after a few days it became more and more obvious that it didn't come at all naturally to him. It was much less trouble to just do whatever his mood told him to, rather than stop and think whether it was the right thing or not. Especially remembering to tell his mother where he was going so she wouldn't have to come looking for him.

The early morning was the most tempting because Mother and Darby were usually sleeping after Shelby's eyes popped open. But today it was afternoon and the same thing was happening. They were both in dreamland, and Shelby was itching to do something - anything! So he quietly left the nest and headed toward the farm to see who else he might make friends with. He remembered to mention Charlie's name if he met anyone new who seemed less than welcoming.

Off he went toward to farm, then through the orchard. He sat for a breather on the   same fence where he had met Sultan just a few days before, and soon his nose started twitching! A mouth-watering aroma was wafting along the lazy afternoon breeze. Shelby didn't recognize the flavour, but he couldn't resist the temptation, so he hopped off the fence and darted in a zigzag pattern toward the nearest building. There was a man in a pen with some really chubby animals who had tiny eyes, large floppy pointed ears, strange snouts with a flat end, and little curly tails. He was cleaning out the feeding troughs and the animals were all lumped together in a corner, some snoozing and others just staring into space. Shelby beat a hasty retreat!

He found himself approaching a house with shutters on the windows and an expansive veranda that wrapped itself around two of the outside walls. The eaves had fancy scrolled patterns cut into the trim that lent a gentle charm to the whole thing. In the yard were several large trees, perfect for observing and where Shelby thought he would be quite safe as he looked around.

He scampered across a tidy yard without any catastrophes, and hastily climbed into the first tree. Up he spiralled and then floated over to a limb nearer to the veranda roof. The aroma was more tantalizing then ever! He was positively drooling by now.

As his gaze focused on the scene below, he found himself noticing a railing that surrounded the veranda, and here and there chairs were grouped with small tables between them. There was nobody about, so he cautiously went along a bough that hung close to the house and launched himself in the direction of the veranda roof. It was so close that he landed softly, where he paused and listened for a moment. All was quiet.

By now he was absolutely positive about the location of the yummy aroma, and quickly climbed down onto the railing, and across it to where two round dishes were sitting in the shade of the tree. He poked his paw into the first one and it collapsed in flakes inward, and exposed a golden filling. Then he stuck his nose in there and flicked into the dish with his tongue.

"Ouch!!" he cried. His tongue was on fire! He scrambled backwards on the railing and sat panting with his mouth open to cool it off.

Then he heard voices from around the corner and he froze on the spot. Oh, no! He was in trouble again, was all he could think.

One of the voices was saying, "I just want to check the apple pies I put on the railing to cool." And immediately a woman appeared, quickly coming straight toward Shelby! He had no time to escape so he jumped onto a table on the veranda and then down underneath one of the chairs. The lady saw him and jiggled the chair, saying firmly, "Shoo, shoo, whatever you are! Go home! Go home!!"

Instead of running, Shelby froze to the spot! She turned to inspect her pies and saw the broken crust, where Shelby had poked it.

"Oh my, you were after my pies!" she exclaimed. Then she bent closer to look straight into Shelby's eyes. "Oh, what a cute little fellow you are! Quite smart, too, if you decided to taste my pies!" at which she laughed gently.

She turned abruptly and disappeared around the corner, slamming a screen door on her way into the house. Shelby got out of there, streaked through the slats in the railing onto the lawn and up into the tree in two seconds flat. He paused to breathe and looked down for a moment.

There was the farmer's wife, carrying a

small bowl which she placed on the railing near to where the pies sat. "There!" she announced in a quiet voice, that reminded Shelby of the nice-looking crossing guard lady. "This is for you! Some apple pieces, much more suited as a snack for a little flying squirrel!" And then she disappeared again into the house.

Shelby heard her voice again from inside, "We have a new animal in the area! A young flying squirrel! He must be one of the group of new residents in our woods that you've noticed. I put some cut apple bits out for him."

Wow, Shelby couldn't believe his luck! What wonderful news he had for Mother and Darby! A place for snacks where they would be safe. Charlie sure knew what he was talking about when he had told them the farm would welcome them.

Down Shelby went, and filled his cheeks with almost all of the cut-up apple. He hurried home where he woke up Mother and Darby and they happily shared the treat from the farmer's wife.

*The pig snorted and replied, "Charlie doesn't come around here! He doesn't include us in his circle of friends! He likes to laugh at us."*

# SHELBY IN THE PIGPEN

It was a few day later, after the adventure that had burned his tongue. Mother and Darby had been amazed at the news that snacks would be put out for them on the veranda railing. Shelby remembered the strange animals he had seen that afternoon and went to take a look. He even remembered to tell his mother where he was going. She had been pretty impressed and said, "Shelby, just be sure they are friendly before you get into that pen. Those are big animals from what you are saying!"

Off he went and soon discovered that Darby was following him. Oh brother, that was going to be the price he would pay for telling his mother where he was going! His sister would be coming along without an invitation! He went faster to try to lose her.

"Shelby, wait up!" she shouted to him, but he ignored her and tore through the trees in the orchard, and dashed full speed toward the pig pen. In a flash it seemed, he was teetering on the fencing around the pen.

Suddenly a dozen mean little eyes were turned his way and a grunting, low-pitched voice said loudly, "Well, what have we here?" and his ample body bumped heavily against the fence. Startled, Shelby lost his footing and fell headlong into the wide trough just below him. He landed in a sea of mush, and felt himself begin to sink into it!

"Help!" he cried. "Get me out of here! Help, someone!"

Meanwhile Darby had arrived at the pen and was looking upon this scene with a horrified expression on her face. Quickly she decided to help and scaled down on the inside of the fence, and jumped onto the edge of the trough.

"Grab my tail! Grab my tail!" she shouted at Shelby. He flailed around and stretched upward as hard as he could and grabbed with all his might, while she hung on for dear life. In a couple of seconds he was perched beside her dripping and smelling terrible. The pigs had been stunned for the moment but now they started to gather around the feed trough, forcing the two flying squirrels to jump away and rush up to the top of the boards again.

The pig that had shaken Shelby off the rail said, "Who are you two and what are you, anyway?"

"Oh, (hic!) we're flying squirrels, and….. (hic!)….(hic!)…." Shelby couldn't get his words to come out, he was so scared!

Darby spoke up bravely, "We just moved into the forest beside the farm. Didn't Charlie tell you about us and all our friends?"

The pig snorted and replied, "Charlie doesn't come around here! He doesn't include us in his circle of friends! He likes to laugh at us."

Shelby was shocked to hear that. Charlie was such a nice horse. He thought about what the pig had said and responded, "But Charlie is so nice to everyone! He laughs at everyone, honestly he does!" Then Shelby remembered Charlie calling him a rat when they had first met and laughing so loudly at his own joke. So he told the pigs all about it.

Then he and Darby told the pigs the whole story about the move and how many others had moved with them. After making peace with each other, the squirrel children took their leave and sat in the orchard to talk things over.

They decided they would just have to ask Charlie about the pigs. They found him in the small paddock behind the barn munching slowly on a mouthful of oats. After saying hello they told him what the pigs had said.

Charlie was outraged! He said indignantly, "They have absolutely no sense of humour! None at all! Everybody else around here can take a joke but they just get all huffy and tell me to scram!"

"Well," began Shelby, "Why don't you explain to them that you don't mean any harm? It's much nicer to be friends. They act as if they don't trust anybody. We felt unwelcome too, but they were okay once we got talking a bit."

"That's right," piped up Darby to help convince Charlie. "They might be able to learn how to be more friendly if you can talk to them!"

So Charlie took off to the pig-pen with Shelby and Darby on his back. As he approached, the pigs turned their backs and were squeezing tightly together in the far corner of the pen.

"Hello, Squealer," Charlie opened. "Please come over and talk to us! I promise I won't laugh. It's a bad habit I have and these two young ones have told me I offended you."

The pigs raised their ears and looked at each

other with surprise. Slowly they turned back around, with Squealer being in the front, obviously the appointed leader.

"You don't think we're ugly and dirty? You don't talk about us when you're with others and tell them bad things? We were so sure that's what you were doing! Everybody thinks pigs are ugly and dirty. It's terrible, and we get very prickly and defensive about it!" he said in a disbelieving tone.

"Honest! Cross my heart!" said Charlie solemnly. "I apologize for not trying harder to be friends all this time!"

After that Squealer and his brood had regular visits from Charlie with Shelby and Darby perched on his strong back, grinning from ear to ear, so glad to have helped patch things up between their new friends. Mother was so proud of them that she let them have a feed of special sweet pine nuts she was saving for a rainy day. Yum!

"You're no friend!! I haven't seen you at all since we moved to this new forest! You've forgotten all about me! What kind of a friend would do that?"

# SHELBY GETS TOLD OFF

Shelby was enjoying a slightly longer sleep on a drizzly morning. He woke up with a jump and flailed his front paws to ward off the flurry of blows someone was raining down on his head.

"Stop! Stop! What are you doing? Leave me alone!" he burst out in a panic. At first he thought he must be dreaming but these blows were real. As he came more awake he could see a small figure darting quickly up and down and back and forth and finally it clicked in what was happening

"Marvin! What is the matter with you? Quit it!" yelled poor Shelby, and gradually the frenzy quieted down.

Shelby sat up then and Marvin, breathing fast, started in, his words tumbling over one another in a mad rush. "You're no friend!! I haven't seen you at all since we moved to this new forest! You've forgotten all about me! What kind of a friend would do that?" he threw at Shelby, with an accusing eye. And he sat back with arms crossed in front of him.

Oh, my, did Shelby ever feel terrible! Marvin was absolutely right. He had lost all track of time and hadn't been playing with any of his friends. He shivered to think of the others coming to show him their disapproval, and said quickly, "Oh, Marvin, I am really, really sorry! Let's go and see everyone and let them all know that I didn't mean to forget! It's just been such a busy time and there is so much to see and find out!"

"Well," said Marvin, backing off, but with a

bit of a self-satisfied tone, "Okay, it will do my heart good to see what the others have to say to you!" he huffed.

So off they went, with Darby trailing along. They couldn't leave her behind very easily. The confrontation had woken her up and Mother was looking on, occasionally nodding her head, as if to say she had expected all this.

The first friends they went to see were Molly and Polly Raccoon. They would soon be fast asleep for the day. While their parents looked on, they told Shelby how they thought he didn't like them any more. He humbly assured them that he was to blame for letting things slide and they made a date to go hunting together that evening. Then they would have a game of tag in the meadow behind the barn, because there would be a full moon.

Heaving a sigh of relief, they continued on, spotting Rosie and Rusty on the next tree. Shelby owned up to his bad behaviour again and promised to visit more often. The baby robins looked almost like their parents by now and that proved how long it had been. Shelby felt so ashamed of himself. Rosie said, "I came over several times but you were never there! We're just glad everything is okay! See you soon!"

That night as the four friends went from tree to tree, with Marvin on Shelby's back, and Molly and Polly running down and up the trunks and Darby and Mother supervising, they were suddenly aware of a large shadow looming overhead, then a flap of wings, accompanied by a WHOOOOO!

With great ceremony, the Wise Old Owl alighted on a branch, blocking their way and sternly cleared his throat. "Well, it seems you might have learned another lesson, young man!" he began. "I am very glad to see you with your old friends at last! Why don't you look around the farm together in future? That way, you will all make new friends together!"

"Oh boy! What a great idea!" they looked at each other and nodded happily. So at dawn the next morning, Shelby took them all to meet Sultan, who paraded them over to the henhouse. "Ladies, these are our new neighbours. Say hello!" A group of brown, cackling chickens crowded around the forest friends. Shelby started introductions, and realized with a shock that Marvin was missing.

At almost the same moment, Sultan came screeching out of the henhouse with a very frightened little field mouse clamped by the tail in his sharp beak. "This rascal was into our feed! He was so busy I caught him without any problem! Where on earth are your manners?" he lit into Marvin, dumping him rudely on the ground.

Marvin struggled to his feet, entirely indignant. "Well, nobody brings *me* food to make sure I don't go hungry! I just realized I haven't had any breakfast! Give me a break, will you!" He stomped his foot for emphasis.

Sultan took charge, with the Wise Old Owl nodding in agreement. He had decided to follow along to make sure things went smoothly on this first joint venture.

"Okay, listen up, you guys!" Sultan said in a

bossy tone. "If you ask, you are always welcome. But helping yourself means the ladies and I will chase you away in a big hurry! So just remember your manners, it's not rocket science!"

So the small group was led to the outside feed trough and happily dug in on one side with the chickens bobbing their heads in their comical, darting way on the other side.

Next morning there were quite a lot more seeds and corn kernels in the trough than usual. The farmer had seen the communal breakfast and was happy to make sure everyone had enough. So every once in a while someone could be seen dipping in with the chickens. They were all becoming friends and it was a nice feeling.

Shelby slept a lot better after that, knowing that he was on the way to being more responsible. Thinking of others gave him a nice warm feeling. Aaahh!

*It had a pair of horns, a stringy little beard, a short scraggly tail, and four skinny legs with pointy hooves at the ends.*

# SHELBY AND THE GRASS TRIMMERS

Off to the orchard went Shelby trailed by Darby, Marvin, Molly and Polly. The raccoon twins were staying awake longer in the daytime so they could play with their friends more often. There were lovely red apples on the trees now and the frisky youngsters would often sit and munch on the fallen ones after a lively game of tag.

Today was no different until suddenly they heard a loud smack and then the branches above them shook violently, causing a shower of apples to come down at them, almost hitting Molly on the head. They all looked around to see what on earth had happened to make the tree shake like that.

There, on the other side of the trunk, was an animal none of them had ever seen before. It had a pair of horns, a stringy little beard, a short scraggly tail, and four skinny legs with pointy hooves at the ends. It was almost snorting as it pawed on the ground, preparing to wham its head on the trunk again.

"Hey!" yelled Shelby at the top of his lungs. Good grief, how many animals had Charlie not spoken to about them moving here? This guy obviously was not running out the welcome wagon! "Why are you doing that? Stop it! Those apples need to wait to be picked, and you nearly bopped us on our heads!"

The beast stopped in mid-snort, and looked with pale eyes at the strange little group in front of him. "I need to get at that spot to chew the grass! I have a job to do here. And you silly creatures are in my way! So shoo, go on, get out of here! Scram!" And he made moves like he would ram the tree again.

"No, wait! Wait a minute!" Shelby pleaded, "Just tell us where you've already done the grass and we can go there with our snack! We didn't mean to make any trouble, and how is it that Charlie didn't tell you about us, anyway?" Shelby got right to the point. This was becoming a regular habit on the farm!

"Okay, that's fair enough!" the other said as he calmed down. "We just got here! Who's Charlie?" He was looking rather confused now.

Oh, boy! Nobody had thought of new animals on the farm that Charlie didn't know yet, either! Okay, so they got down to business and explained all about themselves, then asked without even pausing to think it might be rude, "So what kind of animal are you?" practically in one voice.

"Well, I guess coming from a forest, you've never seen a goat before. Can't blame you for that! Just like I have never been to a forest so how the heck would I know what you guys are all about?" said the goat, just as two smaller goats approached from the other end of the orchard. They had heard all the ruckus and gotten curious.

"Oh, now, here are my two helpers, Nanny and Capra. And my name is Billy." he said quite graciously. "Our job is to keep the grass short in the orchard and around the house. The farmer has enough work to do everywhere else, so this way the grass is taken care of and he also gets milk from these two ladies in the bargain!"

Shelby thought the farmer was pretty smart to have that system going for him. The animals had a good thing and so did the farmer. He wondered how he or his friends might be useful to the farmer and his wife in return for the goodies they were being given with the chicken feed and the fruit snacks on the verandah. That would take some thinking.

Then he had a flash of genius! At least he thought so, anyway. Charlie would know what to do! So off he went to find Charlie. Darby and the raccoon twins followed him like shadows.

Charlie was standing in the shade of an old maple tree by the stable. One back foot was tipped up, resting, and his jaws slowly worked at a mouthful of hay.

He turned his eyes skyward as he pondered the question the little group had for him. Then he took another mouthful of hay out of the trough and went on chewing.

"Well?" spoke up Shelby impatiently, "Do you have any ideas or not? How can we do something nice for the farmer and his wife for being good to us and not chasing us away?"

"Okay, okay, I'm thinking!" responded Charlie, "I don't have to be creative very often, you know! Give an old horse a break here!" And he went on chewing away.

Shelby and his troop sat back to wait it out, looking at each other with little nods. They knew you couldn't hurry Charlie. But it made them itch with impatience!

"Okay," he drawled after a long, long time,

"I think this is a good idea! Did any of you notice the corn stalks, corn cobs, pumpkins and gourds decorating the house and the mailbox and the yard a little while ago?"

They all had and wondered what it was all about at the time. It looked nice, though, and seemed to say something special was happening.

"That was for Thanksgiving." explained Charlie. "But after that is Christmas, and they do it all over again, except it will be pine tree branches and little sprigs of red berries that they go looking for in the woods."

"Oh, we could do that!" said Shelby and the others quickly nodded their agreement. "We should get started right away, shouldn't we? Or do we have to wait again?"

"No, it's coming up quite soon," said Charlie. "I think you could start by deciding where to look first and then when it's time, you'll know exactly where to go in the woods."

So they all agreed that was a good plan and went home satisfied that they could do something the farmer and his wife would like. Tomorrow they would begin!

The next day, they were thrilled to see all the
different things that were trimmed with green and
dotted with spots of red.

# CHRISTMASTIME ON THE FARM

Bright and early on a frosty morning a couple of weeks after Charlie suggested taking pine branches and red berry clusters to the farm for Christmas decorating, Shelby crawled out of the nest and rubbed his eyes. Marvin was sitting there waiting for him!

"Wow, Marvin, you sure got up early!" said Shelby. "Let's go and get Molly and Polly!" And he dashed off upwards with Marvin right behind.

"Aren't you forgetting something?" his voice squeaked behind Shelby's scrabbling toes.

Shelby stopped so fast Marvin ended up on top of his furry tail. "Get off my tail, silly! Ouch!" yelled Shelby. "So what did I forget?"

"ME!" giggled Darby, catching up. Marvin and Shelby exchanged a look and a shrug and resumed their climb. Ten seconds later they were on their way, skimming through the trees.

Molly and Polly were waiting too! Everybody seemed so eager it put Shelby to shame. He could have been sharing every minute with these faithful friends while he traipsed off to the farm by himself. Good reminder to keep in touch!

Off they went and soon each one of them had a pine branch held firmly between clamped teeth. They had to go the whole way on the ground with their loads. Shelby couldn't carry Marvin and the branch. And they needed to stay with Molly and Polly anyways. Marvin struggled valiantly along dragging a leafy frond twice his size.

Halfway though the orchard they had to stop

and rest. Their breath sat in the air in little white puffs. When they set off again the pace was noticeably slower. They were all exhausted by the time they reached the house and carefully put the branches behind the railing where they wouldn't blow away. Then they flopped down on the step wondering whether this was just too big a job for such little animals.

Soon their ears picked up someone laughing, with a neighing whinny. It seemed to be coming closer. What a crazy laugh!

"Charlie!" shouted Darby and Molly and Polly all at once, as if they had rehearsed it. Now they could hear clip-clops as well, and then there he was, in all his horsy glory.

"Nice try! Very nice try!" he smiled at them, when he saw the pile of branches. "Come on, then, up you come! Let me help."

With a burst of fresh energy, they scrambled aboard and grinned from ear to ear at each other as Charlie trotted them off to the woods. They made several trips until the pile was threatening to come over the veranda railing. Charlie deposited the tired bunch at the edge of the trees when the sun was straight overhead and they all went home for lunch.

In the afternoon, the whole routine repeated itself but this time the pile on the veranda was bright red berries, pine cones, and glistening holly leaves. Then they sat back and waited for the farmer's wife to notice what they had done.

The sun was starting to sink toward the treetops, and the sky was turning shades of red and pink when the farmer and his wife drove into the driveway beside the house. How lucky to have chosen a day that shopping in town had to be done! It was worth the long wait to know it would be a real surprise. Now as the couple carried bags of food to the front door, they stopped in their tracks at the sight of the huddled group and the leafy piles on the porch.

"Well, what have we here?" the man exclaimed, looking around in wonder. "These youngsters have brought all of this here and it looks like Charlie must have helped." he observed. "Why on earth would they do that?"

"Oh, for goodness sake!" his wife shot back. "They want to help, and they probably want to say thanks for the food and fruit scraps they are enjoying!" She took a bundle of pine in her arms and clutched a handful of plump red holly berries and went to the door and held them up to it where a wreath might go, nodding her head and smiling.

It looked great just like that, thought the weary crew, now satisfied that they had done the right thing. Her smile was proof enough of that!

After putting the groceries in the kitchen, she returned and covered the two piles with burlap bags and weighted down a few corners to keep everything neatly together. Charlie made one last trip to the forest to take everyone home.

The next day, they were thrilled to see all the different things that were trimmed with green and dotted with spots of red. The mailbox, the railings and the front door. Also the window boxes on the front of the house. The farmer's wife had added large red bows here and there.

That night tiny lights sparkled on the edges of the roof and up the veranda posts. It was breathtaking to the forest children. Shelby and Darby took their mother to the edge of the woods later on to show her how beautiful it was.

She was very proud of her two offspring and made sure she told the others as well. But Shelby took first prize when she whispered in his ear, "You are becoming a very nice young adult, and I am especially proud of you for being the one to decide to thank the farmer and his wife!" Mother was very careful not to play favourites but this time was an exception. Even if it was only a whisper in his ear.

Shelby thought the glow that whisper gave him would last the rest of his life. But the next morning, in her infinite wisdom, Mother gathered Marvin, Molly and Polly and her own twins around her and solemnly stated, "I don't know who had the idea first, but I think all of you deserve to take an equal bow for doing something very kind and thoughtful indeed! Now, let's go and see Charlie so that we can thank him properly for all his help."

That was when they all realized in the blink of an eye that none of them had said thank-you yesterday. They were just too tired! Wouldn't you know, she had thought of that too!

That was when Shelby lost his private glow, and faced the truth that he still had lots he could learn. But he was a happy little flying squirrel, surrounded by treasured friends and family, and all was well in his world.

Soon Santa had found something to give every single one of them for a gift!

# THE MAGIC OF CHRISTMAS

One day late in December Shelby suddenly realized that they would miss Santa's visit to the meadow. And then he started wondering if the reindeer would see the tiny trees before they touched down on their usual rest spot. He decided to ask Charlie if there was anything they could do to bring Santa to this new meadow behind the barn.

Darby had tagged along as was usual now and chattered away as they floated between the trees and then scampered across the barnyard to find the old horse.

"Shelby, we have to find a way to tell them not to go there!" Darby said. "The reindeer could get hurt if they trip when they're landing!"

"I know!" returned Shelby, musing a little about how differently they both were thinking this year. Last year the only thing of interest was how much fun they could have every day. "I don't think the people who planted all those trees will be too happy either because a lot of them will get trampled."

There was Charlie, munching away on a clump of hay. He swung his head around and gazed at the twins as they came closer, then he swallowed with a big awkward gulp.

"What's up, you two?" he asked. "You aren't just over to here to say hello, I don't think!" How on earth did Charlie always know what was happening before it happened? Shelby and Darby exchanged a look and then turned to face him.

In a great burst of excitement, they told

Charlie why they had come over.

"We know the trees are still little, but they won't expect them to be there! Who knows what might happen?" added Darby. "Can you help us, Charlie?"

So Charlie thought in his familiar way, closing his eyes and staying silent until the two flying squirrels began wondering if he had dozed off. They fidgeted and cleared their throats. Charlie blinked thoughtfully. He did everything so slowly! They loved Charlie but he was exasperating at times like this!

Finally, he looked directly at Shelby, then swung his gaze over to Darby and said, "We-ell, I might be able to get a few of my friends together, I mean my horse friends!! If we were to go to the old meadow and spread out, Rudolph would see us and decide not to land. What do you think?"

They agreed that it really was a very good idea. Shelby hoped some of Charlie's friends were light colours, but Charlie said dark  brown and black would show up best on the snow.

"But how can we get Santa to come to our new meadow?" inquired Shelby and Darby together again. That question seemed to have no solution at all.

Off they scampered, shouting a thank-you over their shoulders to Charlie as he returned to his rhythmic chewing.

The next day, Marvin and the raccoon twins were romping with Shelby and Darby and when they paused for a little breather, the Wise Old Owl swooshed down and alighted near them on a swaying branch.

"WHooooo!" he said, somehow sounding wise just with that sound. "What's new with all of my little forest friends today?" He checked on them once in a while, sort of like a kindly uncle.

So they told him about the Christmas Eve plans and hoping to have Santa land at the meadow on the farm instead. He twisted his head around to look at all them all quickly and nodded immediately, saying, "No problem! I'll get my whole family together and lead Santa over there! The horses can do their part and we will do ours!"

And so it actually happened on a starry Christmas Eve that when the magic sleigh circled and slowed over the old meadow, the horses had spread themselves out, and sent up a cheer when they saw Rudolph swerve upward. Then the owls flew close to Rudolph beckoning with their huge yellow eyes. He quickly understood they were there for a reason and followed them, just as they had predicted he would.

At the meadow on the farm, a breathless group waited, watching with wide eyes. Rosie and Rusty were there with their children, the whole raccoon family, plus Marvin and off to one side they saw the Snowshoe Rabbit loping into view. He didn't appear often but here he was, ears flopping away as he approached.

"What in the world is happening? Why is everyone sitting here looking up at the sky? Are you star-gazing maybe?" He had a lot of questions.

They all tried to tell him at once, and after some confusion he sat back and said, "Oh, can I wait with you? I would love to see that, a magic sleigh and a little round man in a red suit!" And he started rolling around on the ground, he laughed so hard.

Just then, there was a flick of a shadow above them. Shelby started running onto the open field and the others trooped after him. The moonlight bathed them in an bluish glow. Then a long whistle could be heard with a downward turn at the end. With a great clatter, their vision was filled with tossing antlers, and flying reindeer hooves. The owl escort regrouped and settled on a low tree branch that hung over the meadow.

The sleigh whisked across behind the reindeer, and gently came to a stop right in the middle of the meadow.

"Okay, team, under the snow is lots of grass to munch on! Break starts now!" announced Santa Claus as he jumped down and started releasing the reins and traces that linked the team together.

The reindeer moved apart and started grazing, making soft tearing sounds. Santa waved the excited group of little friends forward and they gathered in a ring around him. The owls circled for a moment and then perched in a neat row on the high back of the sleigh.

After making a huge fuss about thanking the animals for their help in coming to a safe new meadow, Santa began digging around in his pack.

Just as he raised his head with a specially wrapped parcel for Shelby and his sister, Charlie and his horsy friends trotted up to join the party.

Soon Santa had found something to give

every single one of them for a gift! The Snowshoe Rabbit stared with his jaw dropping at first and then decided he might as well join in. Even the owls received small gifts! That was some magic sack of goodies Santa carried in his sleigh!

Much too soon Santa had to be on his way, and as the sleigh swept by them he called out, "Merry Christmas, everyone! I'll see you here again next year!"

His trailing "Ho, ho, ho!" echoed in the crisp night air and they all knew they would never forget this night!

......*had big beautiful eyes ringed with long lashes, and long wide heads with soft broad muzzles which moved in a slow circles, chewing. Long tasseled tails swished in lazy loops.*

## THE DAIRY BARN

Shelby woke up long before his mother and sister after a winter afternoon nap, just itching to run off on his own the way he used to. He gently shifted himself away from tangled tails and legs and quickly went outside. It was freezing! His breath almost caught in his throat, turning to ice.

"Shelby!! Hey!" came a squeaky voice from below. Marvin! He was jumping up and down trying to keep warm and was about to shout again when Shelby slid down onto the ground beside him.

"Hi, Marv! What's up?" he asked. He spoke in a whisper so Darcy and Mother wouldn't hear him. This was looking like the kind of opportunity he hadn't had for ages. A frolic with his best friend! Once they were a bit further away he excitedly added, "What should we do, Marv? Where should we go looking for new things?" There was still a lot of the farm neither one of them had discovered.

"Well," said Marvin, "there's a building over there, sort of off behind the other barn. I've been wanting to take a look. And we would even be inside, too!"

All Shelby did was nod eagerly and off they went. First they climbed the biggest tree at the edge of the forest and then soared down, Marvin hanging on for dear life but loving every scary second of it. Shelby had learned to fly across to the nearest orchard tree, and they landed fine, but both slightly out of breath with the shock of the cold air.

The sun made long shadows across the

snowy barnyard as they scampered through. Everything was quiet. Even Sultan and his harem had taken shelter from the cold for the night. Shelby and Marvin grinned at each other, already savouring the adventure.

The door was slightly ajar and the lights were on. They approached slowly from one side and then dared to peek in. All they could see was a wall, so in they went and ran quickly behind a post to decide what to do next.

There was no good view from where they crouched so they jumped up on a bale of hay and from there up onto a rail. From there it was a real panorama and what a sight for the two rather tiny friends!

Between similar walls with the rails at the same height were dozens of huge animals. They had big beautiful eyes ringed with long lashes, and long wide heads with soft broad muzzles which moved in slow circles, chewing. Long tasseled tails swished in lazy loops.

A strange hum filled the whole barn. Rows and rows of these immense beasts filled the whole place! There didn't seem to be anyone around so Shelby crept along the top of the rail to get closer. Marvin decided to run along the top on the other side and soon they were eyeing each over the broad back of one of these strange new creatures. It was amazing! That back was even wider than Charlie's! And ended in two bony points just in front of that waving tail.

Nodding at each other they got all the way to the other end and clambered down to the floor.

They both gasped at the maze of black hoses attached to the animals in the stalls. The snaky pattern seemed to actually pulse slightly. Looking more closely, they could see where the ends were attached to each patient animal, so they went looking for the other end.

There lined up neatly in a row, stood gleaming columns of round containers with the hoses slowly filling them. Before Shelby could stop him, Marvin was right on the top of one, pulling at the connection!

It was fastened too tightly to come apart, but soon began to leak and a steady drip began making a thick white streak down the side of the container. Marvin leaned over and tasted cautiously with the tip of his tongue. Soon he was lapping up as much as he could get at, oblivious to the world.

Shelby tapped him on the shoulder to tell Marvin to be careful, and instead scared his little friend so much that he jumped sideways in surprise, managing to lose his balance in the process. He stumbled a few steps to avoid falling over completely and realized he was  much too close to the nearest stall.

Just then the ever-swatting tail connected with a big swoop. Down went Marvin, landing in a heap right between two massive hind legs!!! He struggled up to his feet just as the great beast shifted backward in the stall and brought the heavy black hoses swinging across Marvin's frantic face. He froze on the spot and looked around for Shelby.

"What on earth is going on here?" boomed a stern voice. The farmer suddenly appeared from the next row of stalls, and spotted the terrified mouse. Marvin gave a loud squeak and ran for cover, darting straight between the farmer's legs almost landing in the opposite stall! He changed course, his legs in a mad whirl, and streaked right out the barn door, where he collided with Shelby, and they both collapsed in a shaking heap on the icy ground.

After making sure Marvin was okay, they decided to get out of there fast. But two big rubber boots and a pair of sturdy legs stood in their way. The farmer was staring down at them! Slowly he bent into a squat and placed a small dish on the ground.

"There you go, boys!" he smiled. "Fresh cow's milk. Took you quite a while to find my milkers, didn't it?" He was laughing softly to himself.

Oh, that was a sweet lovely drink! Both Shelby and Marvin knew they would be back here before long.

*Then the children placed a third, much smaller ball on the top, which made the whole thing as tall as the biggest boy!*

# SHELBY GOES DOWNHILL

It was about two months after Christmas and there was still quite a bit of snow on the ground. Shelby and Darby loved to play in it, running about in circles and jumping on top of each other, spraying the white powdery flakes all around. But it was even more fun with other fellow frolickers.

By early afternoon Shelby was wide awake and said to Darby, "Let's go and find some friends to play in the snow!"

Darby was most agreeable; she loved being included in her brother's adventures. He was so good at finding interesting new things to do.

"I'll go find Marvin and you see if you can wake up Molly and Polly," she replied eagerly. Shelby thought that was a clever idea and it meant they would all be together sooner.

The sun was bright as the five friends trotted off towards the meadow, with Shelby leading the way. They played tag for a little while and then flopped back to catch their breath. Shelby sat up suddenly.

"Hey, listen! I hear something!" he said and tipped his head to one side with one ear straight up. "It's over there! Let's go see!"

They knew from experience that Shelby would go no matter what, so they set off together. The sounds led them through a small patch of trees and when they came to its edge they were at the top of a long hill where a group of children chattered merrily. Some of them were at the bottom and others at the top. While the forest youngsters watched, two of the children positioned a long flat thing with a curled-up front and climbed aboard, shoving off with a big push. They went flying down the hill screaming with delight.

At the same time, two others were making their way up dragging a differently shaped item behind them. It was perfectly flat, and sat on two runners, and a rope was attached to one end. The children soon did what the others had done, pushing off with great abandon and soaring perfectly down to the bottom.

A few seconds later, Shelby and Marvin crept a bit closer. Darby and the raccoon kids were right behind them. The children had gathered at the bottom and started throwing snowballs at each other. One of them had left a round red plastic disc at the top of the hill. Soon all the forest friends were lined up along the brow watching the scene below.

Off to one side a bigger boy had taken a sizable clump of snow and was rolling it on the snowy ground. Shelby's eyes popped as he saw the shape grow into a large white ball. Soon the ball was half as high as the boy pushing it! Abruptly, he left it and began another. Two of the other children had gone to a fresh patch to start a ball of their own. Then they rolled it over and the big boy lifted it up and placed it on top of the first one.

"What are they doing?" Darby wanted to know. "They must be building something!"

"Oh, look now, here comes another one!" said Molly as the children placed a third, much smaller ball on the top, which made the whole thing as tall as the biggest boy!

The children seemed to wander off after that. Shelby turned to say something to Marvin and noticed he had climbed onto the red plastic disc.

Marvin explained, "My feet were cold and at least this isn't covered in snow!" So Shelby joined him and sat down to relax for a few minutes. Molly, Polly, and Darby went scampering off to the nearest fir tree to play tag in the feathery branches.

"Let's go and play tag too!" said Marvin suddenly, jumping over the edge of the red disc. Shelby felt it move and then start to slide. In a blur it was at the very edge of the hill and gathering speed! It slipped over the brink and raced down, down, down with the frightened flying squirrel hanging on for dear life.

"Shelby!!" screamed Darby. "Watch out!!"

But there was nothing anyone could do. The red disc was headed straight for the big piled-up snowballs. There was a squishy crash and snow flew everywhere as Shelby ended his wild ride. Everything toppled over and the red disc spun off on its own. Shelby lay dazed on the ground.

The children came running and one of them yelled out, "Our snowman! He's ruined!!" They gathered around poor little Shelby, who was sitting up and trying to clear his head.

"You poor little guy!" one of the little girls said quietly, which made Shelby turn and look at her. By then Darby had raced down the hill to help her brother. The other three followed close behind.

"We better move out of the way," said the very wise little girl, "or he'll be too afraid." So they backed away and watched as Darby rushed up to Shelby and helped him get onto his feet.

The children could see that he was going to be alright, so they raised a cheer as a shaken little squirrel crept away from the demolished snowman. He felt much better very soon, so at the top of the hill he turned and looked down. The children were climbing up too, bringing the disc, the sled and toboggan.

The little girl who had spoken put the toboggan down and pointed to it and at the animals to ask if anyone wanted to ride down with her. Marvin and Shelby decided quickly that it would be fun now that there was nothing at the bottom to crash into.

Away they whizzed while Darby held her breath and Molly and Polly ran back and forth to show how worried they were. *Honestly, boys have no sense!* they thought. But before they could blink, the little girl had towed the toboggan back up the hill with Shelby and Marvin grinning from ear to ear!

It was such a wonderful afternoon, the rest of it spent with all of them taking turns on the front of the toboggan. And they were all so tired that night they slept right through, missing the night hunt altogether. Marvin finally appeared under the squirrel tree half way through the next morning. Molly and Polly slept so long they missed lunch! Mother was rather upset and wouldn't let either Darby or Shelby out of her sight for the next several days!

*All he could see was buildings, glass, and sidewalk.*

# SHELBY GOES TO TOWN

It had starting to warm up nicely the last few days. The sun had melted away all the snow, and the whole forest seemed to be full of new life. Darby had found some green shoots in a sheltered spot peeking through the layer of dried leaves and pine needles that had lain there all winter. Mother said that meant it was Spring for sure.

Marvin and Shelby were playing with the raccoon sisters, while Darby had stayed at home with Mother relining the nest with clean pine needles. Suddenly the stillness of the usually quiet woods was shattered with a  loud chugging sound, and a lot of rattling noises. Shelby and his friends climbed quickly to a strong oak branch to be able to see what the disturbance was all about.

A few moments passed with the racket getting louder and closer, and then through the low bushes under the oak tree burst a bright red truck with three men sitting in the open back and two in the front.

The truck slowed sharply to an accompaniment of squeaking brakes and the men jumped out. The one who had been driving said, "Okay, now listen! We have to do some pruning of these bushes here to make room for the small evergreens that have self-seeded. The shoots are there, but they have no chance of making it without some light and more space."

Soon they had moved off into the trees, taking saws and clippers with them. The sounds of cutting and snipping drifted back through to the clearing. Above, the curious animals looked at each other and then moved down the massive trunk to get closer to the truck. That's when Marvin stuck his nose in the air and piped in his high voice, "I smell something good!"

He led the way, but Shelby was right on his heels. Molly and Polly hung back to see what would happen. They remembered being in cages last winter and being brought to the old forest in a truck a lot like this one. Nothing could have made them get any closer, not even a tempting smell of good things to eat.

In what seemed like no time, Shelby had his nose inside a bag that was sitting on the floor in the back of the truck. When he brought his face back up his eyes were dancing with glee. "It's peanuts!! Come on and get some! There's lots of time to run away if they come back because we will hear them. C'mon, Molly! It's OK, Polly! I'm not afraid, and neither is Marvin!"

Polly climbed into the cab at the front and Molly joined Shelby. Marvin thought he better see what Polly was up to. She had found a small case on the seat, and had pulled a round orange ball out of it. It had a new aroma but it was a very nice one.

She and Marvin started gnawing at the skin and didn't much like it, but right under that skin was soft juicy bright orange fruit with a wonderful sweet taste. Pretty soon they were both smacking their lips and had a lot of juice dribbling down their chins.

They were so engrossed in the delight they had discovered they didn't hear the men approaching. The driver was at the door shouting, "Hey! Get out of there! Look, those two are into our oranges!! What a mess! There's juice all over the seat!"

Shelby froze in the back of the truck, too shocked to move, and much too late realized that tools were being tossed in, almost landing on him. Molly moved quickly and hid behind the bag where the peanuts were. Shelby could feel the eyes on him, or he thought he could, so to hide he wriggled inside the bag and dug his way to the bottom. He heard Molly jump to one side and leap over the side and he already knew that Marvin and Polly had been able to leap through the opposite window and plop heavily on the ground together before streaking off into the protection of the bushes and trees. They sat with Molly as the men jumped back in.

"We can do a little more tomorrow, guys," said the driver, "and thanks for the help today. We can have a few decent Christmas trees here if we look after them while they grow."

The doors slammed shut and the motor roared to life, and soon there was only a lingering smell of fumes and the wheel tracks to show that it had ever been there at all.

Shelby knew he was in trouble when the truck started moving! He also knew there was nothing he could do. Three burly men were sitting so close to him!!

After what seemed a lifetime to Shelby, the truck pulled to a stop and all the men left. They filed into a nearby door, saying, "I'm in need of a sandwich!" and "Nuts! I'm having a steak!" and "Thanks for offering us lunch! We brought our own, but this is much better!"

Shelby stuck his head out of the bag and looked around. All he could see was buildings, glass, and sidewalk. And people walking along looking in the windows.

He crept to the edge of the truck bed where the men had left the tailgate open. And jumped down to the sidewalk in a flash. Run! It was all he could think of doing.

So that's what happened. He ran along close to the edge of the sidewalk and then darted down an alley, to get away from all those faces. It was darker in the alley and he headed for the light at the end and rounded the corner, looking from side to side.

To his right he could see a big dog tied up, and decided it would be better to go the other way. He darted toward a trash can and sat behind it to catch his breath. Then he heard voices coming his way.

"Guess we better get back to the farm," said a man, "before it gets much later. Too many things to do while there's daylight." Shelby ears twitched! That voice was so familiar.

"Fine by me!" replied a woman's voice. "I have baking to do."

Shelby peeked out and, and sure enough, it was the farmer and his wife! He couldn't believe his eyes. So he followed along and jumped into the car when the doors were open, dodging behind the farmer's back when he turned.

It was easy to hop out at the farm because both the farmer and his wife went to the trunk to unload, and Shelby raced frantically for home. The welcome he got was quite a spectacle! Molly, Polly, their parents, Marvin and Mother and Darby were so happy to see him they started dancing to celebrate.

Shelby always knew his friends and his family liked him, but that night he knew they all loved him very much!

*He sat regally, long neck arched, wings circling his body in a glorious display of long white feathers. And he could glide without a ripple along the surface of the water.*

# SHELBY GOES SWIMMING

It was finally full summer again. The whole world seemed to buzz with activity. Green and yellow fields lay under the smiling sun, and the days were so much longer it was no trouble at all finding time to play. On a lazy afternoon, Shelby and Marvin had gone searching for mushrooms in the woods, and found themselves on the far side where they had gone tobogganing not so very long ago.

They tumbled down the hill and raced across the flat field at the bottom, then stopped in their tracks as a tall white bird came running at them, wings flapping furiously.

"Shoo!" it shrieked in a honky voice. "Go away!" Then it proceeded to actually hiss at them, so they backed up a little and sat down in a bit of a shock.

The creature stopped hissing and waving and stood looking down at them. It stood on quite sturdy black legs and its feet were flat. The smallish head sat on the top of a long gracefully curving neck. Beady eyes, above a narrow orange beak, glared down at the two helpless friends.

"You better not stay around here!" the thing admonished them, "You're nothing but trouble for us!"

"Please, Mr Bird, we were only having fun! Why can't we play here?" Marvin got the nerve to speak up first.

"Bird? Bird?? I'm no ordinary bird. I will have you know I am a swan! Try to remember that.

Swans are not ordinary birds, let me tell you!"

"Will you tell us about swans?" Shelby asked, finally finding his tongue. "We want to learn and we aren't trouble at all, honest!" And before he could stop himself he blurted, "You have the strangest feet I've ever seen!"

Mollified by the honest curiosity, the swan said in a much more civilized tone, "They're for swimming, you silly thing! Don't you know anything?" And with that he turned and strutted awkwardly away. It really seemed he was inviting them to follow so that's what they did.

Through a few small shrubs the swan pushed, and went straight into the pond that sparkled on the other side. Instantly, he was transformed into the most beautiful sight either Shelby or Marvin had ever set eyes on. He sat regally, long neck arched, wings circling his body in a glorious display of long white feathers. And he could glide without a ripple along the surface of the water.

Shelby was so awed, he forgot to stop at the pond's edge and he found himself suddenly in the water! He started to panic and splashed wildly around, only to succeed in getting more wet and further from the shore. Marvin stood watching with his heart in his mouth, not knowing what to do.

Shelby had swallowed a few mouthfuls and gone completely under by the time two swans nudged him toward the shore where he found his feet on the bottom and scrambled out spraying water everywhere. He sat down, shaking off the last drops and looked around for Marvin.

"If you want to swim," he heard from nearby, "you need to calm down when you are in the water! You'll float along just fine if you stop behaving like a windmill!"

Actually, the water had felt wonderfully cool after running in the heat of the day. So Shelby thought it over. He was still sitting on the bank when Marvin splashed toward him, laughing with glee. "Come on in! It's easy, it really is!" and darted easily away toward the centre of the pond.

Shamed now, Shelby had to do something to show he was no coward. He stuck one foot in and then another and waded carefully forward. Marvin called out, "Just keep your feet moving and your nose up!" and to his utter surprise, Shelby found he was swimming. Not as gracefully as the swans but he was swimming nonetheless.

The two swans had gone off a short distance and now they were back with a whole long string of miniature swans behind them. The little ones were covered with fluffy gray down, but in every other way they were as beautiful as their courtly parents.

Soon, they had all made friends and spent the rest of the afternoon splashing in and out of the pond. Then Marvin and Shelby lay in the sun to let their fur dry off, and before very long drifted off to sleep. They were awakened by a hubbub of flapping and hissing. The two adult swans were out of the water facing a new animal. It was covered in a thick white coat, had a black face, small quivering ears and rather mild eyes that were looking none too happy.

"Baa-aa-a!" it bleated piteously at the swans, "it's OK, please quiet down! I just got here today, so I don't know my way around!" and the poor thing continued to shake under their haughty wrath.

Shelby jumped up and shouted, "Why don't you try saying hello first? Maybe you can make a friend instead of scaring everyone off without knowing anything about them!" at which the swans looked a little surprised and stood together facing the new arrival.

"Well, then, hello and who are you?" the mother swan wanted to know.

"I'm a sheep! Well, actually, more like a lamb, and they call me Olive. I just came to this farm on a truck today with some other lambs. I don't know how I got lost, but here I am, just trying to find the rest of the group I came with." and she looked from side to side to wait for a reply.

The slightly embarrassed swans apologized for over-reacting and wished Olive a good day, then hastily made their way back to the pond where their babies were cowering together waiting.

Shelby said to Olive, "If you need to go to where the barn is we can help. We've lived here for almost a year now, so we know most of the animals too."

They set off together, heading back towards the barn. Marvin hopped on Shelby's back for a while, but was quite content to jog along on his own too. Olive wasn't in a particular hurry. She took her time explaining that her coat would be growing all the next winter and it would be sheared in the spring for making wool.

Soon they were joined by three more young sheep, who had been turned loose in the orchard, and were contentedly grazing on the lush grass, in company with Billy and his two ladies, Nanny and Capra. Olive was so happy to be back with the others, she fairly leaped with joy.

She called after Shelby, "I hope you will come to talk soon! Thanks for helping."

And Shelby knew he had grown up a bit more because he was just happy to do something nice for no reason at all.

*Shelby felt strangely attracted to the sweet smile of the sister. Her name was Petra Flying Squirrel.*

## SHELBY MEETS HIS MATCH

Shelby was swimming in deep water, with no shoreline in sight, and someone was yelling his name so he was struggling to find a way out. The shouting persisted, and then a gentle touch on his shoulder brought him into his warm bed, and there were Mother and Darby looking on with worried expressions.

"Marvin is calling you! Wake up!" Mother said urgently. "You were dreaming! Marvin needs us."

Darby poked her head out of the nest hole and waved at Marvin. "Just a minute, he's awake now!" she called to him.

All three of them scurried down the trunk, Shelby still feeling a little groggy. "Whatever is the matter? You're here even earlier than usual, Marv," said Darby.

"A whole family of flying squirrels is in trouble at the old forest! We have to go and help! Come on!" was his breathless reply.

They quickly decided to stuff some food into their cheeks before setting off. As they went soaring through the treetops, with Marvin staying quiet for once, they wondered what could have happened.

When they came to the edge of the trees, they had to go along on the ground for a while. Marvin said, as he ran along puffing a little, "The Wise Old Owl told me to get you. Your old nest tree finally split open! And a family of flying squirrels is trapped right now!"

Mother said, "That crack in the trunk always made me a bit nervous. This could have happened to us!!" Shelby and Darby exchanged a look, realizing they were lucky to have moved when they did.

As they got closer to the fallen tree, they could see Ringtail and his family waiting. The Wise Old Owl sat nearby.

"We need you to squeeze in under those branches and see what is happening. Marvin, maybe you could lead the way since you are the smallest. There is no space for me or Ringtail to get through." he said with a flutter of his huge wings. "I'm glad I flew over here today, and heard them calling for help!"

So Marvin and Shelby started to squirm under the tangle of boughs toward the split tree trunk where it lay at a sharp angle. Everything had come to rest on a nearby oak with sturdy spreading limbs. But thick branches almost obscured the nest hole altogether where the two trees had become intertwined.

"Can you hear me?" Shelby called out. "Can you move?"

Three voices responded all at once, quite unintelligible. After a short pause came one, "We are okay, but there is just too much covering the opening!"

When Marvin and Shelby were close enough to see, they realized it would take quite a bit of strength to shift the twisted mess enough to free the family. Wise Old Owl flew by saying, "I'll get Charlie! Just wait for us!" Shelby thought how lucky they were to have such good friends.

While waiting they were able to find out that the cowering family in need of rescue had come and moved in only two months before, and for the same reason that Shelby's family had moved there almost two years ago. Their spirits were clearly raised to hear about the lovely woods beside the farm and all the good things the forest animals had shared since settling there.

Soon Charlie clip-clopped into view and in no time he managed to push his strong shoulder into the leaves and shift the debris aside, exposing the crushed opening. Three anxious faces peered out.

Everyone pitched in then to clear a little more and eventually three very grateful flying squirrels crept out to safety. The brother and sister were the same age as Shelby and Darby!

When they reached the forest by the farm, Rusty and Rosie flew out to meet them. The new arrivals received a warm welcome from the whole circle of friends.

It was time to introduce everyone. The flying squirrel mothers did the honours. Shelby felt strangely attracted to the sweet smile of the sister. Her name was Petra Flying Squirrel, and her brother was Peter.

"We know a perfect place for a nest!" offered Shelby, feeling very gallant. So the whole troop followed him to a tree right in the centre of the woods overlooking a tiny clearing with clusters of blackberry bushes. Then he and Darby and Mother emptied their cheeks to offer the newcomers their first meal. After that the younger ones flew back and forth several times between the two nests carrying a good portion of the stored nuts to begin the supply that all flying squirrels keep on hand. The two mothers busied themselves lining part of the hollow tree with soft cedar and feathers they collected during a diligent search.

The next day the new friends gathered in the orchard. After meeting the goats and sheep, who were munching contentedly under the apple trees, they all went to see Sultan and his broody hens. Petra backed up when Sultan pranced toward them.

"It's okay! He's big, but he's our friend!" Shelby assured her quickly. After that she seemed to stay rather close to him as they continued on around the farm. Shelby noticed that Peter and Darby were chattering together comfortably as they went along.

Marvin kept reminding them how many more animals they could meet and tried to hurry them up a little. Molly and Polly had to go home to sleep. They had missed the night hunt after yesterday's excitement and wanted to be awake later.

It was late afternoon before Petra and Peter had met Squealer and his fellow oinkers. It was decided that the dairy barn and the swans would have to wait until another day.

Charlie ambled over to see how things were going. He nodded sagely to himself, seeing how very nicely everyone was getting along. He trotted through the forest as the squirrels floated happily back toward the new family's nest, with Marvin

148

firmly attached to Shelby's back.

Both mothers were still there, making the finishing touches on the nest lining and patting a few more nuts into place on one side. Charlie spoke from below and they climbed down to greet him. "Well," he said, "it looks a lot like Shelby and Darby might have just found their mates. What do you think?" he asked.

It was agreed that he was probably right and that next spring, being grown up and ready, two pairs of adult flying squirrels would be busy building their very own nests in nearby trees.

Mother sighed deeply and said to her new friend, "That would make me very happy! Very happy indeed!"

Milton Keynes UK
Ingram Content Group UK Ltd.
UKHW050011290824
447448UK00019B/285

9 781988 972015

The Shelby F. Squirrel Series
BOOK ONE

The
COMPLETE
Adventures of

# SHELBY F. SQUIRREL

and Friends

Eleanor Lawrie

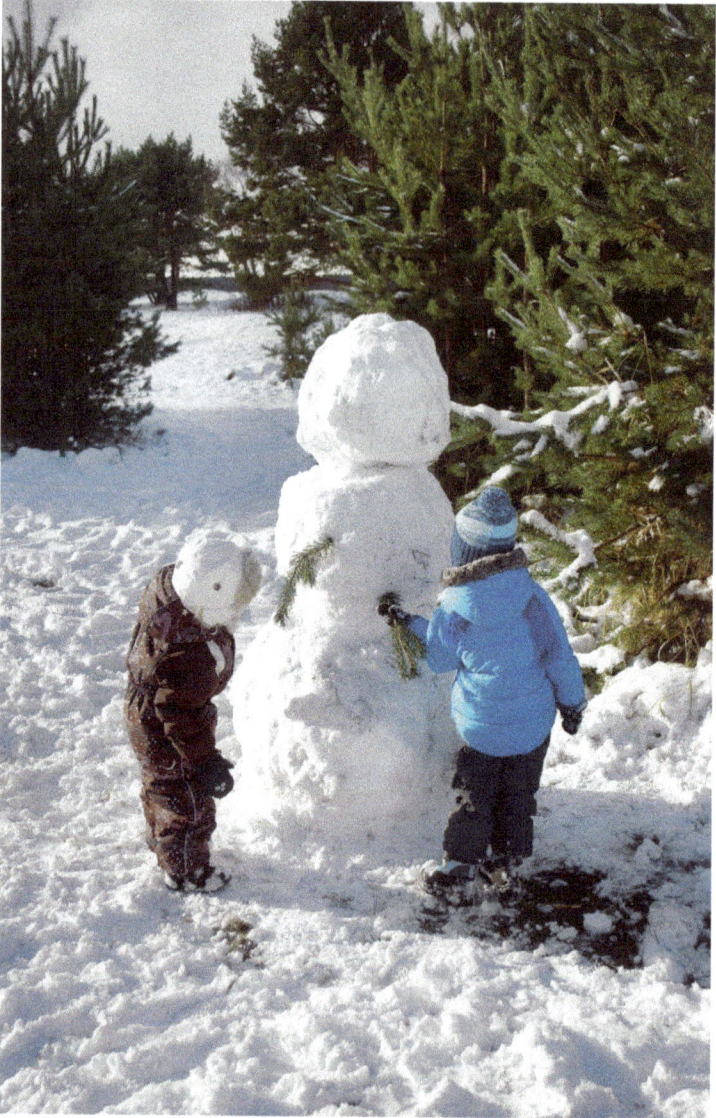